Hi Ne

I d

the book. Please

leave any feedback on

my website.

Pll

Heygood Gambit

Edited by Michelle Josette
FictionEdit.com

ISBN: 9781728787121

Heygood Gambit

[Fastball Series]

A Legal and Financial Thriller

PHILIP BECK

To my family and friends who encouraged me to
write the second book in the *Fastball Series*.

PROLOGUE

My life was finally back to normal after the wild ride last summer caused by the fallout from my former friend Jack Heygood's involvement in a Ponzi scheme at now-defunct Tropical Investments. Jack avoided federal prison time by testifying against his former partners but couldn't escape the disgruntled investors who lost millions of dollars and wanted street justice and their money back. Many people, including his family and friends, were drawn into the swirl of unethical behavior, questionable business dealings, illicit sexual relationships and murder that always seemed to surround him. After being captured in an alligator-infested canal in Boynton Beach, Florida, Jack was later sentenced to the Texas State Prison for shooting up an affluent North Dallas neighborhood.

All of my tranquility quickly ended after Tropical kingpin William Clayton's conviction was reversed by an appeals court and Jack parlayed his promise of testimony in the retrial into a release from prison. Several years ago when we coached baseball together I thought I knew Jack well. Now, I didn't know what he was capable of doing.

CHAPTER 1

Beginnings by Chicago started playing on my iPhone when the alarm went off. I didn't want to get out of bed and pulled the blanket over my head. Soon Maggie snuggled up behind me and gave me a hug. Her warm body was very comforting. Maggie is my best friend and lover who moved in with my son Joe and me a few months ago. Although in her mid-forties, she still has her tall and lean cross-country build from college with shoulder length brown hair and blue eyes. We were friends for a number of years before we got much closer this past summer. She is the District VP of a large pizza chain and we frequently get laughs swapping work stories.

"Lonny, I want to tell you how much I have enjoyed living with you and Joe. He's like the son I always wanted."

"He hasn't seen much of Joan since she walked out years ago. So your motherly attention is very much appreciated by both of us."

I rolled over on my back and kissed Maggie. She smiled and climbed on top. Her hands gently held my face as we passionately kissed. Then she looked into my eyes and said, "I want to spend the rest of my life with you."

"Oh oh oh oh woah woah woah—" I responded.

Maggie frowned and interjected, "Stop that—you can't sing and even got the lyrics wrong. I'm being serious."

Then Maggie leaned in and kissed me. I whispered in her ear, "Oh Maggie...I feel a hundred different feelings...that sounds wonderful."

Maggie shook her head and smiled. "Finally, that's what I wanted to hear."

As Maggie straddled me, she started unfastening the buttons on my pajama top. We locked eyes.

"Maggie, did you just propose to me?"

A mischievous smile appeared on her face. "Yes, and you just accepted."

Maggie looked down at me as her hands felt my chest. I needed her now.

Bang, Bang, Bang.

Someone was pounding on the door.

"Hey Dad, get up, the next news report is about Tropical Investments. Something about an appeals court in Georgia."

Maggie and I quickly put our pajamas back on and joined Joe in front of the television in the kitchen as the orange juice commercial ended on CNN.

"This is Steve Johnson reporting from the United States Court of Appeals for the Eleventh Circuit in Atlanta. Today, the court overturned the conviction of former Tropical Investments CEO

William Clayton citing prosecutorial misconduct. The Federal Prosecutor failed to turn over key evidence to Clayton's defense team. William Clayton was the poster boy for white collar crime after he and other insiders orchestrated a Ponzi scheme and the investors lost millions of dollars. He had been sentenced to twenty-five years in prison after been being convicted on thirty-three counts. Just minutes ago, I had a chance to get a reaction to the court's decision from Assistant Attorney General Al Stephens."

Then the previously recorded interview with Al Stephens started to play.

"Mr. Stephens, what is next for William Clayton? His previous trial cost the tax payers five million dollars. Do you plan to release Mr. Clayton or put him on trial again?"

Stephens grimaced and narrowed his eyes. "First and foremost, we completely disagree with the court's decision today. In my opinion, the Federal prosecutors followed the spirit and letter of the law in this case."

He paused briefly and glared at the camera.

"Second, putting white collar criminals in prison is a top priority of this administration. We will do whatever it takes to make sure justice is served. We owe that to the American people."

CNN went to a commercial and Joe turned to Maggie and me. Then his eyes widened.

"Didn't Jack Heygood testify against William Clayton at his trial?"

"Yeah, Jim Taggart did some legal research and felt that Jack's testimony against Clayton kept him out of prison."

Joe shook his head. "So Jack was a rat."

"Probably so, but never say that to Mark."

CHAPTER 2

Skip Wise, VP of Corporate Development at National Airlines, and I headed upstairs to the Planning Committee meeting on the seventh floor. All of the senior executives would be there. At least this time, we were on the agenda and had time to prepare a presentation on project Green Field—the potential acquisition of Global Airlines' East Coast slots and routes to England. Northern Airlines, our number one competitor, was also vying to acquire those assets and had already met several times with Global. My financial analytics team supported the negotiations by pricing out the various purchase agreement proposals being discussed. This work included using machine learning capabilities in the cloud to forecast passenger demand on the new international routes and the resulting incremental demand in our domestic network; plus building financial models to evaluate the overall economic benefit to National Airlines.

Skip was thirty years old, stood a little under six foot, and weighed a scrawny one hundred, sixty-five pounds. His neatly coiffed hair was cut weekly. He had risen rapidly through the ranks of the finance department after joining National as an analyst upon completing his MBA.

We walked into the CEO's conference room and all of National's senior executives were already seated around a large oval conference table. There were white boards on all of the walls and coffee was brewing on a table to the right side of the double doors. CEO William "Bill" Wolf and President Daniel "Dan" McAfferty were seated next to each other and engaged in a side conversation. We sat down in the two empty seats to the left of Dan. Bill was almost ten years older than Dan but you wouldn't know it from their appearances. Bill's light brown hair was slicked back, probably through the use of some hair product, while Dan had a very full head of thick, gray hair.

Skip fired up the presentation but waited for Dan and Bill to finish before he started. Dan and Bill turned and faced the group. Skip took a deep breath and started, "We have an update on Project Green Field that—"

Before Skip could say any more Bill Wolf raised his hands and looked around the table as the smile left his face. "Gents, our progress on Green Field hasn't been acceptable. Northern always seems to be one step ahead of us—almost as if they know our next moves. The negotiating session with Global in Fort Lauderdale fell apart after Northern beat us to the punch and sent their team to New York."

Bill Wolf paused briefly and slammed his fist on the table. "We have to do better!"

Dan McAfferty, with a cigarette in his hand, interjected with his very deep voice, "Bill, you're absolutely right. We will do better."

There was an eerie silence as Dan scanned the room and made eye contact with each of the senior executives.

Bill flashed his large, glistening white teeth. "What is particularly upsetting is that Northern's latest offer is only slightly sweeter than our proposal. We are going to keep a much tighter lid on our negotiating position going forward."

Dan turned to Skip. "What are your next steps?"

"Lonny Jones and I are doing a conference call with Global in a couple of days. Hopefully, we will get some constructive feedback on our proposal—"

Bill Wolf scowled and screamed, "Those bastards at Global are trying to create a bidding war between us and Northern to drive the price higher."

Dan took a puff from his cigarette and turned to his left. His face was only inches away from Skip. "Goddam it Skip, make something happen."

Our time slot was up and we left the Planning Committee meeting without making our planned presentation on Project Greenfield. But we had our marching orders. As we got into the elevator for the ride down to the fourth floor, Skip sighed and said, "What a beatdown! If we don't make progress soon I could be toast."

I shook my head. "Let's grab some lunch at Los Bobos in Grapevine."

Twenty minutes later we were headed north on State Highway 360 in Skip's 1987 dull-red Alfa Romeo Spider Graduate. The top was down and the wind rushed over our heads. The car was best suited for someone a foot shorter than me. I turned to Skip and yelled over to him, "If you're keeping this soup can to pick up older women, you'd be well-served to put a fresh coat of wax on it."

Skip laughed and stepped on the accelerator.

CHAPTER 3

Los Bobos, located on the edge of historic downtown Grapevine, was a few miles north of National Airlines' headquarters and a frequent lunch destination. The restaurant had fifteen tables, each with a well-worn, yellow plastic table cloth. Cheap Mexican curios lined the shelves that ringed the establishment. A five-page menu offered a variety of tasty options but Skip and I would always choose between the Mexican chicken fried steak and the carnitas. We never looked at the menu but just made a game-time decision when the waiter came to take our order. Today was no different. Seated at a corner table with a parking lot view, Skip and I were recapping our earlier visit to the Planning Committee to discuss project Green Field when the waiter arrived.

"Señores, are you ready to order?"

Skip nodded. "I'll have the carnitas."

I looked up and paused. "Ahh—"

Skip interjected, "You're on the clock Jones."

Then Skip started banging his hand on the table. "Five, four, three, two—"

"Ok, ok, give me the steak."

We both laughed but the waiter rolled his eyes and shook his head as he had seen this performance many times before.

Then we jumped into the chips and salsa.

"Do you like the verde sauce more than the roja?" inquired Skip.

"Both are great but I sure could use an iced tea to put out the fire. Where's the waiter?"

We looked around but he wasn't to be seen.

In a couple of minutes my phone started to vibrate and ring. People seated at the adjacent table seemed to be amused by the *Rockford Files* ring tone. The call was from a number I had never seen before. I glanced at Skip. "Probably a salesman, I'll let it ring."

"No, take it. The call could be important," said Skip with a laugh.

I answered the call. "Lonny Jones here."

"Mr. Jones, this is Max Siebel, Jack Heygood's attorney."

I shook my head in disbelief and looked across the table at Skip before I responded. "Huh, why is Jack Heygood's attorney calling me now?"

"Jack would like to see you."

I didn't have a fond memory of Jack Heygood. Over the course of the last year, I had been sucked into the swirl of problems and violence that seemed to surround him after Tropical Investments filed for bankruptcy protection three years ago and the bankruptcy court examiner, with the help of the FBI, determined that a small cabal of insiders had orchestrated a Ponzi scheme and defrauded investors out of hundreds of millions of dollars. Jack, as Senior Vice President of Marketing, was a player in the inner circle at Tropical but managed to escape jail by providing testimony for the government at the trials of his co-conspirators.

He thought he was out of the woods by avoiding jail but the defrauded investors had other ideas. To many investors, Jack was the face of Tropical Investments since he marketed the investment opportunities to them and convinced them to invest. They thought Jack was still sitting on some of the money generated by the scam and were willing to go to great lengths to get their money back. If Jack took a beating in the process then so much the better. I mistakenly tried to intervene in one altercation between Jack and a couple of thugs in the parking lot at a youth baseball game. Once I arrived on the scene, Jack used that distraction as an opportunity to escape and left me to battle the thugs alone and barely avoid getting my hair parted by a tire iron. On another occasion, Jack was being tailed and decided to take refuge in my Phoenix hotel room to avoid detection. Unfortunately, he led his pursuers right to my room and I woke up in the middle of the night looking at the business end of a sawed-off shotgun. Earlier this year, Jack was sentenced to the Texas State Prison due to a shootout in an upscale residential neighborhood in North Dallas. Three men were spotted digging up a suitcase in the backyard of Jack's former house and, when confronted, fired at Lt. Vince Truex of the Dallas Police and myself. Over fifty shots were exchanged in a wild gun battle that was the talk of Dallas for several weeks. Jack was finally apprehended weeks later after a high-speed police chase through Boynton Beach, Florida that ended when he drove his truck into the alligator-infested Stanley Weaver Canal.

"What? Why does Jack Heygood want to see me?"

"He was recently transferred to the Walls Unit. You are already on his visitation list. Would it be possible for you to drive down to Huntsville this Saturday for visiting hours?" said Max Siebel matter-of-factly.

"I thought I had seen the last of Jack Heygood after they pulled him out of the canal in Florida and he went on trial for shooting up a fashionable neighborhood in North Dallas. We were close years ago when we coached our boys' baseball team but now that's just water under the bridge."

"Mr. Jones, my client denies any involvement in the shootout on Strait Lane with you and Lieutenant Truex. He has no idea who the three men were that exchanged gunfire with you. His reputation has been unfairly sullied by that incident."

I shrugged my shoulders. "I don't know if I will meet him, let me think about it."

"Jack knows how you feel and requested I talk to you only because this matter is of the utmost importance."

I gripped the phone tighter. "I'm not promising anything."

"One last thing, Jack wanted me to inform you that your help could lead to a very lucrative opportunity. Thank you for your time and I hope you give this request careful consideration."

I laughed for a moment. "Does Jack want me to drive the getaway car in a bank robbery?"

"No. I look forward to hearing from you. Good day, Mr. Jones."

As I hung up the phone, Skip looked over at me and laughed. "Unbelievable."

I dipped a chip into the verde sauce. "Yeah, Jack is pretty ballsy so I shouldn't be too surprised."

"Be careful, you had a pretty wild adventure in Delray Beach last year—staking out Jack's apartment, almost taking a shower with a hooker and the police chase."

"The only reason I would give Jack the time of day after all of the problems he's caused is because Joe and his son Mark are great friends—he stayed with us last summer when they both played on the Generals 17U (seventeen and under) baseball team."

"Yeah, I remember; that was tragic when Mark's mother was killed and Jack was living the good life near the beach in Florida with his bimbo girlfriend and nowhere to be found."

I looked over to Skip just as I started to dig into my Mexican chicken fried steak. "I don't know what I'm going to do."

Skip finished chewing a mouthful of carnitas and then wiped a spot of sauce off the corner of his cheek. Skip shook his head. "Don't do it. Don't do it. Stay away from that dumpster fire at all costs."

CHAPTER 4

Inmate visitation at the Walls Unit was eight to five on weekends. To avoid the mid-day rush of visitors, I left Dallas for Huntsville at six in the morning. Interstate 45 southbound was wide open at that hour so I set the cruise control in my Dark Highland Green, 2008 Mustang GT *Bullitt* to eighty miles per hour. I hoped to make the one-hundred-and-sixty-mile trip in two hours.

What was I doing visiting Jack? I tried to help him last year but got burned every time. He only cared about himself. Even though I knew this trip was a mistake I kept driving south. Maybe I was doing this to help his son Mark. Many different thoughts raced through my head as the time passed.

Soon the Eleventh Street exit in Huntsville appeared so I exited the highway and headed east towards downtown and the Walls Unit—the oldest facility in the Texas State Prison System. The high, red brick walls that surrounded the Walls Unit were easy to spot. The visitor registration center was on Twelfth Street so I went around the block and parked in the visitors' lot adjacent to the front of the main entrance. Per prison regulations regarding contraband, I left my cell phone, laptop, and wallet with paper money in the trunk of my car and then walked up a flight of stairs to enter the prison carrying only my driver's license, car key, and a small plastic bag carrying two dollars in quarters in case I wanted to buy something from a vending machine. A metal detector manned by three guards was ahead of me. After passing through, I was patted down by a guard. The mandatory paperwork was easy to complete because of the information Jack's lawyer provided in a follow-up conversation. I found a seat in the waiting room and looked around at the emotionless people sitting around me.

Thirty minutes later a burly guard stood up at the front desk and announced, "Leroy Biggs, Lonny Jones, Olivia McFarland and Jorge Tatis, Sr., please come with me."

A door was unlocked and we walked into the visitation center. The walls were dark grey and the overhead lights were bright. Ten prisoners could receive guests at the same time. Jack was already seated towards the left of the room on the other side of a thick, bullet-proof glass window and waved to me as I sat down. We both picked up a telephone so we could communicate. The guard turned to us just before he exited. "You have thirty minutes."

Jack was tall, around 6'2", with brown hair, a dark complexion and deep-set dark eyes that were contrasted by his white prison uniform. He looked thinner than I remembered him in Delray Beach several months ago.

We stared at each other for a few moments and then Jack nodded. "Lonny, have you ordered a new 2019 *Bullitt*—four hundred seventy-five horsepower, top speed of one hundred and sixty-three, and Recaro seats?"

"Jack, I don't think you invited me down to Huntsville to discuss cars. What do you want?"

Jack cocked his head to the side and grimaced. "I need a favor."

I straightened up in my chair. "After everything I went through last year as a result of your shenanigans, why should I help you?"

Jack paused for several seconds and looked down. He shut his eyes and flattened his mouth. Then he looked up with his eyes opened wide. "Because you're my friend."

I didn't know if I should laugh or cry and just stared at Jack for a few seconds. "It depends; what exactly do you want me to do?"

"You heard the Appeals Court in Atlanta threw out William Clayton's guilty verdict?"

"Yes, we saw the announcement on CNN."

"The DOJ is not going to let Clayton walk—they have to put him on trial again."

"Based upon what Assistant Attorney General Al Stephens said on TV, that wouldn't surprise me...So just what exactly do you want me to do?"

"They needed me to testify before and they need me to testify now if they want to convict Clayton. I want savvy representation to get the best deal—I want to walk."

"Ok, so just how do I play into this?"

Jack leaned forward until his face was just inches from the thick glass window that separated us. "I want your friend Jim Taggart to represent me.

Taggart has the moxie to go toe-to-toe with Al Stephens."

"Taggart's practice is focused on business law—helping distressed companies and mergers."

Jack raised his hands and opened his mouth. "Don't you remember the Willie Drumingo case twenty years ago?"

"Yeah, we watched that unfold on national TV while we were sitting at a bar after a golf game. How could I forget?"

Jack leaned back in his chair and smiled. "If Taggart could save Drumingo then he can get me outside of these red brick walls."

I chuckled to myself—I should have figured that Jack was going to work some angle. "I will talk to Jim but I don't think he will touch your case."

Jack nodded. "All I want you to do is try."

I raised my hands with the palms facing Jack. "Ok, ok, but that's all I will do."

We stared at each other for a couple of minutes. I leaned back. "Jack aren't you going to ask how your son Mark is doing?"

Jack winced and looked up at the ceiling. "Oh yeah, he won't respond to my letters because he thinks I was responsible in some way for his mother's murder."

I shook my head up and down. "That crossed my mind too."

Jack fidgeted in his chair. "I had nothing to do with Wendy's murder."

"Let's talk about something else," I suggested.

"Ok, great, will Mark and Joe play together on the Dallas Generals baseball team this summer?"

"General Manager Mike Rizzo came to the house a couple of months ago—both Mark and Joe are on the team."

Jack sighed with relief. "Great."

"In fact, they are going to play an exhibition game over at TCU in a couple of weeks."

Jack looked up. "Does Mark have any chance of getting a baseball scholarship? What have you heard?"

"Nothing recently since Mark moved to Oklahoma City to live with your sister Sharon. Last summer, he reached out to a lot of programs but received form-letter responses."

"Who's he contacted?"

"If I remember correctly, a few schools in the Ivy League, most of the Big 12 and one or two in the ACC."

Shaking his head, Jack said, "I didn't like his approach at the plate last year—not aggressive enough. I wish I could have played a role in his life the last couple of years and coached him up. I could've been throwing batting practice."

I leaned back in my chair and listened.

"Do you remember those years when we used to throw BP all afternoon in the cage in your backyard?

I smiled. "Yeah, good times."

"I really miss it. That was fun—probably the best times of my life."

Jack's eyes narrowed. "If things go as planned, I'll be able to catch some of the action next summer and find a path back to my previous lavish-lifestyle in North Dallas."

I shook my head as Jack continued, "Lonny, don't forget to look at the 2019 *Bullitt*, it's coming out this summer."

"I won't."

Jack smiled. "You're a shade tree mechanic and

like to tinker with your old car but you deserve the best."

"Yeah."

Jack raised his eyebrows. "If you get me out of here, I'll buy you one this summer. I am going to be awash in cash and I will help my friends."

The metal door opened and a guard entered. "Your thirty minutes are up. Heygood, you're going back to your cell."

We both stood up and our eyes met. "Lonny, I'm counting on you to talk to Taggart."

"I'll give it a shot but I'm not promising he will represent you."

"Fair enough," said Jack as he was led out by the guard. His prosthetic left arm was barely visible underneath the long sleeve of his white prison uniform.

● ● ●

Race traffic near Ennis brought Interstate 45 to a standstill thirty miles south of Dallas. Finally, I pulled into my driveway at three o'clock. Maggie walked out the front door and headed in my direction. She looked particularly stunning today.

"How was your trip?"

I gave her a hug and then we walked towards the front door.

"Jack never ceases to amaze me. He thinks he can parlay Clayton's overturned conviction into his release from prison."

Maggie put her hands on her hips. "Really?"

"He wants Jim Taggart to represent him in the negotiations with the Attorney General's office."

"Why Jim? I thought he did mergers and

acquisitions."

"Jack still remembers the Willie Drumingo case."

Maggie had a quizzical look on her face. "What was that about?"

"Drumingo was convicted of murdering two girls in Southern California twenty-five years ago and was sentenced to death."

"How was Jim involved?"

"Jim grew up in the Bay Area and went to law school at Berkeley. He was a product of that environment and thought the criminal justice system wasn't fair. He used to do pro bono appeals court work on select criminal cases when he first moved to Dallas."

"He represented Drumingo?"

"Yes. Jim obtained a last-minute stay of execution. It was pretty dramatic and drew a lot of attention. Jack and I watched the live news story unfold over lunch at a golf course bar."

"What happened?"

"The Warden of San Quentin and Jim were both interviewed on CNN. According to the Warden, Drumingo was strapped down in the gas chamber and the door was sealed."

Maggie's eyes widened. "So it was a close call?"

"The call from the appeals court judge came in at nine-fifty-nine and the cyanide pellets were going to drop at ten. Drumingo is the only condemned man who has walked out of the gas chamber."

Maggie scrunched up her eyebrows. "So Jack was impressed. Do you think Jim will take the case?"

"Good question. Jim told me that his team was working all weekend to prepare for a deposition on

Monday. I'll give him a call next week."

CHAPTER 5

Sunday morning was beautiful for early December in Dallas—not a cloud in the sky and fifty-five degrees. The golf bag was in the trunk and I needed to practice. My short game needed work after my last disastrous outing. I put the car into reverse and slowly started to back down the driveway. Then *Whump*! That damn cat Toots jumped onto the hood of my car and looked at me face-to-face through the windshield. My ex-wife Joan abandoned her demanding cat when she walked out and moved in with her boyfriend years ago so now Toots, a large orange tabby, was my problem to deal with. I turned off the engine and got out to pick up Toots from the hood and put him on the lawn. I ignored Toots' needy meowing, got back in the car and continued down the driveway. Suddenly, a car appeared out of nowhere with its horn blasting and pulled into the driveway at a high speed blocking my exit. A woman exited the car and walked towards me. I quickly recognized the figure; it was my ex-wife Joan. What a terrible way to start the day!

Joan and I had been married for fifteen years. Then she had an affair with her boss and moved out. At forty-six, Joan was starting to show her age with wrinkles around her eyes and added weight but back in the day she had been a vivacious looker and party girl. When we were divorced I was granted sole custody of our son Joe and she didn't ask for visitation rights. Joan was very emotional and a loose cannon so I never knew what to expect.

In seconds, we were facing each other in the middle of the driveway between our two cars.

"Hello, Joan. What do you want?"

Joan batted her eyes and placed the palms of her hands on my chest. "Lonny, I have been thinking about us."

Her eyes darted back and forth and she started to breathe heavily. Since she left me years ago our conversations were always short and to the point without any physical contact. Usually, she had a caustic tone. Today was different. I shook my head in disbelief. "C'mon Joan, cut the bullshit."

Joan took a step closer. "You gave such a beautiful speech at Wendy Heygood's funeral. It was very kind and I knew then that I wanted to get back together with you."

I chuckled. "Joe told me that you and your boss, I mean boyfriend, Hal, are not together anymore. He left you for his twenty-something secretary? I guess the miles started to show and he traded you in for a new model. That's the reason you're here."

"Oh no, I want to tell you what I really feel about you."

I backpedaled and held up my hands with the

palms facing Joan. My neighbor across the street stood in the middle of his driveway with his arms folded and listened intently to our conversion.

"In my front yard! Look around. The neighbors are outside. For God's sake. You're creating a spectacle."

Joan glanced from side to side. "Huh."

I took another step backwards. "It's a little late for that, we both have moved on."

Joan's face reddened and she gritted her teeth. Raising her voice, Joan said, "We had something special those first few years. I know I screwed it up when I played around with Hal."

"Yeah, you sure did—"

"I've changed and I want you back."

"You want me back because Hal dumped you and you don't have any options."

I looked around—the neighbors on both sides were now taking it all in. This scene was an embarrassment to me. Then Joan took two steps forward and cocked her head sideways.

"Lonny, that's not true. You are my true love."

"Well, I'm not available. Maggie and I got engaged last week."

Joan's face turned bright red and she screamed, "What!"

"Yeah, she's a wonderful woman and I am lucky that she will have me."

Joan started waving her arms. "That bitch! You're making a huge mistake. We'll see about that."

"Don't make any problems."

The neighbor across the street blurted out, "Is everything all right over there? Should I call the police?"

I looked back at her. "Louder Joan, then

everyone on the block can hear you!"

Joan glared at me as she walked to her car. Just then Maggie's Jeep Cherokee pulled up and parked on the street in front of the house. Maggie got out and was soon a few feet away from Joan.

Joan grabbed Maggie by the arm. "Just because you're playing house with Lonny doesn't mean you'll ever get married. Lonny and I had something special. You are just a milquetoast accountant without a figure. What could he possibly see in you?"

Maggie freed herself from Joan's grip and pushed her away. "Joan, you are a good-for-nothing tramp."

In seconds, I was standing between them and turned to Joan. "Get out of here."

Just at that moment, Toots appeared and started to meow. Joan looked down. "Oh Toots, I've missed you."

Then Joan reached down to pick up Toots. He hissed, swatted at her outreached hands, and ran towards the backyard.

Joan clinched her teeth and walked to her car. Soon she sped away as her tires screeched.

Hopefully I had seen the last of Joan for a while. I decided to postpone my practice round of golf and walked back into the house with Maggie to try to smooth out the awkward confrontation with Joan.

CHAPTER 6

It was after quitting time at National Airlines and I merged the Mustang into the east-bound traffic towards Dallas on State Highway 183. This was a good time to call Jim Taggart to discuss Jack's request so I flipped through my contacts and dialed his office number. Jim was a managing partner at a prestigious Dallas law firm and a long-time friend. The receptionist answered, "Hello, Frazier, Smith, Sturdivant and Taggart, how may I help you?

"This is Lonny Jones, Jim Taggart please."

"One moment, I am connecting you now."

A few seconds later, I heard Jim's booming voice, "Hello, Lonny. What's up?"

"Are congratulations in order?"

"What?"

"The last time I called, the firm was named Frazier, Smith and Sturdivant."

Jim paused briefly. "Oh yeah, I generated fifty percent of the firm's revenues last year so they want to keep me around. My practice keeps forty-five lawyers busy and billable. We are involved in litigation across the country."

"Congratulations!"

"So, what can I do for you?"

"Remember our buddy Jack Heygood?"

"Oh no."

"Yes. At the request of his counsel, Max Siebel, I visited Jack in Huntsville on Saturday."

"What precipitated your visit?"

"You will not believe this—he wants you to negotiate with the Justice Department on his behalf."

"Ah, so Jack thinks he's holding a few wild cards after the Appeals Court in Atlanta threw out William Clayton's conviction."

"That's exactly right; he thinks you can secure his release."

Jim laughed. "The man has some chutzpah! I don't handle criminal cases anymore. My focus is on helping distressed companies reorganize and enabling mergers and acquisitions."

"But you once did."

There was a brief pause. "That was over twenty years ago. Representing poor scumbags does not support my opulent lifestyle," said Jim with a sarcastic laugh.

"Jack still remembers the Willie Drumingo case. We saw it unfold live on national TV over lunch at a golf course."

Jim remained silent for thirty seconds and then his voice took on a very serious tone. "Oh yeah, I remember. The Drumingo appeal work caused me to stop practicing criminal law."

"What? I never heard that before."

"After Drumingo was resentenced and moved from death row to the general population, he killed a guard and another prisoner. I spoke to him just before he was transferred to Pelican Island and asked if he killed those two girls. He started laughing and said he enjoyed hearing them scream and beg for their lives."

"Wow."

"I thought he was being railroaded by a young, overzealous district attorney named Al Stephens. In retrospect, I should have gone out for a cup of coffee and donuts that morning instead of hurrying to the appeals court. Drumingo should have been gassed."

I didn't know what to say so I paused for several seconds. "What should I tell Jack?"

"Tell him he doesn't have enough money to afford my services."

"Will do. Sorry to bother you with this Heygood stuff."

"That's ok."

"We need to catch up. How would you like to come over for dinner next Saturday? We would love to see you."

"Sounds good. It will be nice to see Maggie and Joe. See you then."

CHAPTER 7

I was still processing my conversation with Jim Taggart when I pulled into my driveway. Maggie stood outside and walked towards me, beaming. When she got closer she seemed to study my expression and the smile left her face. "Is everything alright? You look out of sorts."

"I spoke to Jim Taggart. He no-bid the negotiation with the feds."

Maggie nodded. "I am not surprised. What did he say?"

"He was burned badly on his last pro bono gig— the Drumingo appeal. Drumingo confessed that he killed the two girls and had no remorse. He laughed in Jim's face."

Maggie shook her head. "Oh my!"

"I don't think Jim has gotten over it after twenty years. I wonder if I am the first person he shared that story with. It was tough for him to get it off his chest."

Maggie and I walked through the front door into the living room. Joe sat near the front window watching TV. Maggie looked at me. "What's Jack going to do now?"

"I don't know. It's Jack's problem now."

"By the way, your dad called. He's coming over in a few minutes,"

"That's great. I wonder why? Did he say?"

"He visited his doctor today and wants to talk to you."

"I hope everything is ok."

Joe turned and glanced out the window. "Grandpa Pete is here."

Joe opened the front door and gave him a hug as he walked in. Even though he was my father, I sometimes called him Pete, like everyone else, when we joked around. Pete's hair was white as snow. He was in good shape and could still pass as a firefighter ten years after he retired. But his face was ashen gray today. He walked over to Maggie and gave her a hug. Then he turned and slapped me on the back. He appeared to be in good spirits. What did his doctor tell him? Pete looked around and the smile disappeared on his face. "I saw the doctor today...we discussed the test results."

"What tests?"

Pete lost his breath and quickly sat down on the couch. Maggie glanced over at me and had a concerned look on her face. I turned to him. "What did the doctor say?"

"Well they took some blood last week and did a PSA test."

I asked, "The prostate cancer screening test?"

Pete shook his head and briefly looked down. "Yes, my score was elevated. The doctor thinks I may have cancer and he needs to do more tests."

"Oh no," said Maggie.

Pete leaned back and sighed. "They want me to do an MRI on Wednesday at two."

"Then what?" I said.

"If the MRI detects problems the doctor will do a biopsy next week. The MRI guides the biopsy."

I felt so bad for Pete. He looked devastated. "Dad, I will go with you to the MRI."

Pete looked over at me and briefly smiled. "Thank you, son."

"Let's meet here at noon on Wednesday and I will drive you to the clinic."

"That sounds great. I can't eat anything after midnight before the test."

"We'll grab some lunch afterwards. Maybe at that little hamburger joint you like."

Pete smiled, gathered himself and walked to the front door. "Thanks, son. See you on Wednesday."

Then he turned and waved as he walked out the door.

CHAPTER 8

Wednesday came quickly. Pete Jones pulled out of the City of Dallas Fire Station Thirty-Five onto Walnut Hill Lane. The visits back to the station broke the boredom of retirement and kept Pete connected to the people he had worked with for thirty years. Fifteen minutes later he pulled into Lonny's driveway at eleven-thirty. As always, Pete was early. There was no sign of Lonny's Mustang *Bullitt* but a white van was parked on the street directly in front of the house. Pete walked up the sidewalk towards the front door. As he got closer, he noticed it was ajar. Maybe Maggie or Joe was at home?

Pete opened the door and looked inside. "Hello, is anyone home?"

There was no response. Then he heard someone walking down the stairs.

"Joe, is that you?"

Pete took two steps toward the stairs. Two men

were descending the stairs. The one in front was taller and balding while the second man had jet black hair and carried a tool box.

"Hey, who are you? What are you doing?" said Pete as he stared at the two men.

Pete blocked the path to the front door. In seconds Pete was face-to-face with the taller, balding man who had a smirk on his face and was chewing gum. The second man was heavy set and looked like a weightlifter.

"Why are you here?" demanded Pete.

Looking down on Pete, the taller man said, "Old man, there are a couple of ways we can do this. You can get out of the way nice and easy or you can go through the spin cycle and get a rock shampoo."

At seventy-two, Pete was a stubborn guy who still worked out.

"I'm not moving until you tell me what you're doing."

The taller man grabbed Pete's shirt just before he let fly with a left hook that landed on the right side of the taller man's head. The man winced in pain and then threw a punch that landed squarely in Pete's chest sending him flying backwards. Pete landed in the middle of the wooden coffee table hitting his head and breaking the table into two pieces. The two men quickly ran out the front door as Pete lay moaning on the floor. He struggled to get up but fell down and passed out.

Fifteen minutes later the mailman walked up to the mailbox located near the front door and peered inside. The police arrived five minutes later. "Mr. Jones, Mr. Jones can you hear me?"

"Yes, I can," responded Pete as he lay on the ground holding his chest.

"Mr. Jones, this is Lieutenant Truex, Lonny's friend. Do you remember me? I heard the address on the police radio and came over as quickly as I could."

Pete smiled and looked up. "Vince, nice to see you!"

Truex kneeled down to be closer to Pete. "The ambulance will be here soon. Please tell me what happened."

Pete started breathing hard. "There were two men. One of them carried a tool box. The other's hands were free."

The Fire Department ambulance pulled up in the driveway with its siren blaring. An attendant quickly jumped out and ran over to Pete. As he put an oxygen mask on Pete, he said, "No more questions; we need to get this man to the hospital."

The ambulance sped away and Vince picked up his cell phone and punched in a number. "Hello, Lonny. This is Vince. Your dad is on the way to the hospital. He walked in on two intruders in your house."

CHAPTER 9

As a precaution, the doctor held Dad overnight in the hospital for observation despite his protestations. Visiting hours were over so I headed home. Vince Truex's car was parked on the street in front of my house. I turned the Mustang into my driveway and walked over to his car.

I had known Vince for over twenty years. Vince stood 6'1" and weighed 190 pounds with blackish hair and a dark complexion. His rock-hard physique had been toned through a daily workout regimen. We lived in the same sprawling, singles apartment complex off of Greenville Avenue when I started working in Dallas at National Airlines in the mid-1980s. He shared an apartment with three other rookie officers directly across the hall from me. We were all single and enjoyed the night life. The parties at their apartment were legendary and always attended by many attractive female residents. That's where I met my ex-wife Joan.

I extended my hand to Vince. "Thanks for coming over earlier when you heard about the burglary."

Only half of Vince's face was illuminated by the street light. Vince first looked towards the house and then gazed at me. "I'm not sure it was a burglary."

"What do you mean?"

"Maggie and Joe have looked all over the house and nothing appears to be missing."

"Really?"

"Nothing looks like it has been touched. Maggie's jewelry was visible in the bedroom but everything is still there."

"Dad has been sleeping at the hospital so I didn't have a chance to talk to him. What about you? Did he say anything?"

"We talked before the ambulance arrived. He said the two men were not carrying anything except the shorter man held some sort of tool box that Pete had never seen before."

"Lonny, do you have any idea why the two men were in your house?"

"Hmmm, something just occurred to me. This could be a stretch. The execs at National Airlines think there has been a security breach around a secret acquisition project that I've been involved with over the last several months. Our competitor seems to have inside information."

"So, you think National was investigating you?"

"I don't know. Last year we had a problem with a high-level executive—some people thought he might have been involved in some illegal activities. There was a rumor that a private security firm was brought in."

"Which firm? I know all of the local guys."

"No, they're not local. Veritas Associates is based out of Langley."

"Langley?"

"Virginia."

"Are these company guys?"

"Yeah, the rumor is that most are ex-CIA with a few former Special Forces types."

"Really?"

"Supposedly, they not only find leaks but plug them if the money is right."

Vince's eyes widened. "Oh, wow. They're in a whole different league."

"I overheard a couple of the senior guys talking last year. One jokingly said that you ask them what they found out but never how they found out. The other guy became very flustered when he realized their remarks had been overheard."

"Does Veritas Associates have an ongoing relationship with your company?"

"That's an interesting question. A friend of mine who is in accounting heard some of these same rumors. She checked our financial system and there is no record of any payments from National to Veritas Associates."

Vince had a concerned look on his face. "What happened to the high-level exec that Veritas investigated?"

"It was strange. He was forty-five years old and in perfect health but drowned in his hot tub. The doctor said it was a heart attack."

Raising his eyebrows, Vince paused for a moment. "I wonder if Pete surprised them installing surveillance equipment in your home or hacking into your computer?"

"Are you talking electronic bugs?"

Vince leaned against his unmarked Dallas Police car. "Could be. The department doesn't have the advanced capability to sweep your house, but I have some friends in the Dallas FBI that could help. Maybe they have some information on Veritas too. Let's not mention any of this when we are inside your house."

Vince and I walked into the house, picked up a couple of cold beers from the refrigerator and then headed to the patio to unwind after a very long day. After finishing the first beer, I turned to Vince. "I have an interesting Jack Heygood story for you."

Vince exhaled. "What's he up to now? I thought he was a guest of the Texas Prison System and tucked away where he couldn't create any problems."

"Haha. Never underestimate Jack!"

Vince grimaced and popped open another beer.

CHAPTER 10

Skip and I planned to discuss our next steps on Project Green Field over breakfast at National Airlines. So I headed west on State Highway 183 thirty minutes earlier than usual. Traffic started to slow east of MacArthur due construction and then my cell phone started to ring and I answered the call.

"Lonny, this is Vince. I talked to some of my friends over at the bureau. Veritas Associates is a wholly owned subsidiary of McAllister Support—a firm with many government contracts, that's basically a paramilitary outfit. They market themselves as mercenaries outside of the country and a discrete investigative operation in the United States."

"Really?"

"They are a no-nonsense outfit that shoots first and asks questions later. If they come back to your house, don't engage. They are heavily armed. I recommend you start carrying a concealed weapon. You have the permit, right?"

"Vince, thanks for the uplifting news! I appreciate the call."

"One other thing, my friends at the bureau will be able to sweep your house for bugs tomorrow afternoon at three o'clock. Does that work?"

"Yes, I appreciate your getting that set up."

"Your house could be under surveillance so we'll come incognito."

"Ok, is there anything I need to do before you come?"

"Check around to see if anything is out of place. For persistent surveillance, the bugs need a power supply. Look at your power strips and outlets that are out of sight behind furniture."

"Will do."

"Also, look for new wires and USB cords and anything new connected to your router."

"Ok."

"If you find anything then write what you found and the location on a piece of paper that you can hand to us. Don't say anything that could be picked up by a bug."

"Thanks, see you tomorrow."

● ● ●

Skip arrived at the cafeteria before me and was already eating when I went through the checkout line and paid for my two eggs over-easy, toast and coffee. He was seated with his back to the windows and beckoned to me. Skip did not have the customary smile on his face, rather he looked tired and on edge.

"I heard Pete was attacked yesterday at your house. How's he doing?"

"Dad has a mild concussion and was kept overnight at the hospital for observation. I plan to pick him up after work today."

"Did anything valuable get stolen?"

"Surprisingly, nothing was taken. Maggie's jewelry was on the dresser in clear sight and not touched. Pete told me that one of the men was carrying a tool box that he had never seen before. The other guy wasn't holding anything."

Skip put his fork down and his face became expressionless. "That really sounds strange."

I took a couple of sips of coffee and a bite of my eggs before responding. "Detective Truex came over last night. I told him about the senior guys thinking there is a mole here at National who is feeding information to Northern about our negotiating positions."

Skip's eyes narrowed. "What did he think?"

"That certainly got his attention. I mentioned the rumors about the company using Veritas Associates last year."

Skip gulped. "You think the company brought in Veritas Associates to find the mole?"

The eggs needed a little seasoning so I reached for the pepper. "Maybe. Truex called me this morning. He made some phone calls. Veritas Associates is a wholly owned subsidiary of McAllister Support, a firm the Army hired to do work in Iraq. Sort of a private army that did dirty work that the Army didn't want to do."

"Wasn't that the outfit that lost their contract after the Congressional investigation...because they used excessive force and killed twenty civilians for no reason."

"Yeah, that's it."

Skip's face got red and perspiration dripped from his forehead. "Wha, wha, what's going to happen?"

I took a couple more bites of the eggs and washed them down with a big gulp of coffee. "Maybe they think I'm the mole. Truex thought they might have planted surveillance equipment at the house."

Skip started to breathe hard. "Geez, what happens if they think we're leaking? Are we going to drown in a hot tub? I don't even have a gun."

Skip threw his napkin on top of his half-eaten plate of food, abruptly stood up and quickly walked out of the cafeteria. I continued eating and headed to my office ten minutes later.

CHAPTER 11

I left work early and pulled up in my driveway at two-forty-five. My earlier review of power supplies and connections to computer equipment didn't turn up any evidence of bugs so it would be up to the boys from the bureau to figure it out. A few minutes after three o'clock, a blue van pulled into the driveway behind the *Bullitt*. The sign on the side of the van said, "A & B Painting Co.—the *Ph.Ds.* of Painting." Three men wearing painter's attire emerged from the van and started to unload drop clothes, brushes, step ladders and other painting supplies. Soon they were at the front door and rang the doorbell. I opened the door and was face-to-face with Vince Truex wearing a "We Cover the Earth" tee shirt. Vince smiled and said, "Mr. Jones, we're here to paint your bedroom."

"Thanks for coming," I responded.

"I know you mentioned earlier that you might want us to paint several other rooms. If you like, show me around and I can provide an estimate."

"That sounds great."

Vince glanced at the stairs. "First, let's get my men set up in the bedroom."

We walked up the stairs and entered the master bedroom. The two men with Vince started to unload electronic equipment hidden in the painting supply buckets. A "radio frequency detector" label was attached to the side of one device. One of the men started scanning the master bedroom while the other agent with a small hand-held device followed Vince and me around from room to room as we made small talk.

Vince and I stepped out on the back patio while boys from the bureau moved slowly and methodically from room-to-room and scanned for bugs. After thirty minutes, one of the men emerged from the house and joined us on the back patio. He looked at Vince and said, "There's one bug attached to the light below the ceiling fan."

Vince nodded. "Good work. Let's take a look."

We followed him up the stairs to the master bedroom. The other agent stood on a step ladder and was taking apart the light. He pointed at a blue wire that connected a small silver microphone—the size of a dime—to the power supply for the fan.

For a moment I paused and thought about the situation—how my privacy had been violated by this intrusion. What would Maggie say when I told her that our intimate love-making session last night had been shared with some ruthless strangers? I motioned to Vince to follow me and I headed back out to the patio.

"You are going to take the bug out, right?"

Vince shrugged his shoulders. "I don't know. It

may be advantageous to feed these guys bad information and enable us to arrest them."

"That's not going to play well with Maggie."

"I'm sorry but this may be our best hope to catch them."

Vince walked back inside while I sat out on the patio and waited for the agents to complete their sweep. Time passed slowly as I surfed the internet with my phone. The sweep continued for another forty minutes before one of the agents walked outside with Vince.

Vince sat down on an adjacent chair. "We found a camera and microphone embedded in the back of the bookshelf in your office."

I glanced at the agent. "So they know you're here and sweeping for bugs?"

The agent grimaced and nodded affirmatively. My eyes shifted to Vince. "So what are you going to do about the bugs and camera?"

Vince sighed and looked at the agent. "Kill 'em."

CHAPTER 12

Jim Taggart parked his Mercedes 450 SL on the street in front of the house and walked up the sidewalk to the front door. He was in his mid-forties and had black hair with a little gray near his ears, and walked with a slight limp due to a surfing accident at Zuma Beach close to the northern end of Malibu several years ago. Jim was a California boy who frequently talked about returning home after he retired from his legal practice in Dallas. His dream was to get a place on the ocean. Jim rang the bell twice and Maggie answered.

"Jim, so nice to see you. I love your Hawaiian shirt. Come on in."

Jim briefly put his arm around Maggie. "Thanks, I bought it off the rack for one hundred and eighteen dollars so it better look good!" Jim said with a smile.

Maggie and Jim both laughed and Jim walked into the living room. I rounded the corner from the kitchen. "Jim, what can I get you to drink?"

Jim grinned. "A very dirty martini would be nice."

"How many olives? The usual three?"

"Yes, of course, with plenty of juice. Thanks."

I glanced over at Maggie. "What are you drinking?"

"I'll have a glass of merlot."

Maggie and Jim sat down on the couch as I returned to the kitchen to make the drinks.

Maggie turned to Jim. "How's life treating you?"

"Work is hectic. I feel like a salesman. I have to spend eighty percent of my time generating new business for the firm rather than working on litigation."

"Lonny said you are a named partner so you must be doing a great job. Sales isn't always fun—"

Jim interrupted, "Yes, but it drives everything else."

Maggie leaned back and smiled. "Did you hear the big news?"

Jim raised his eyebrows. "No, what?"

"Lonny and I are engaged!"

"Congratulations, when did Lonny propose?"

Maggie winked at Jim and he erupted in laughter.

"Haha. I knew it—you took matters into your own hands."

Maggie blushed as I returned with the drinks.

Jim grabbed his very dirty martini. "Lonny, why am I not surprised that Maggie proposed to you?"

"Why don't you guys enjoy your drinks instead of giving me a hard time?"

We had another round of drinks before we moved into the dining room. After a few minutes, I went out to the patio and took the steaks off of the grill while Maggie brought out the salad. Soon we were seated. Jim took a bite of the steak. "This steak is delicious!"

We were five bites in when the doorbell rang twice. "Who could that be?" said Maggie.

I wiped my mouth, walked over and opened the door. To my surprise Mark Heygood and Jack's sister Sharon stood on the front porch. Mark's eyes were red and his hair disheveled. He had his father's dark complexion and deep-set eyes. Sharon appeared exhausted and her face was expressionless.

Sharon looked directly at me. "Lonny I am sorry to bother you and arrive unannounced at your house during the dinner hour but we visited Jack in Huntsville today and he needs your help."

The smile quickly left my face. "What does he want now?"

Mark Heygood took a step forward. "Mr. Jones, my dad wants you to talk to Jim Taggart again."

Maggie and Jim heard the conversation in the dining room and exchanged glances. Jim shook his head in disgust. "Jones, was this dinner a setup?"

I raised my hands and shook my head. "No, no. I had no idea."

As I stood at the door looking at Jim, Mark and Sharon walked right past me into the house.

Jim stood up and glared at them. "I'm Jim Taggart."

Mark walked over and stood directly in front of Jim. Tears started to flow down his cheeks. "My mother is dead. I need my father. Please help me!"

Jim's jaw dropped and he said nothing. Sharon took a step forward. Her voice cracked. "Mr. Taggart, I am so sorry to bother you and drag you into this.

But we're desperate, we need you to represent Jack. He thinks you are the only one who can get him out. I am begging you. Please help us."

Jim looked around in disbelief. He was in an unfair position. I stepped in between Mark and Jim. "Ok, ok, you have made your points. Please show Mr. Taggart some courtesy and leave now."

Mark and Sharon both gazed at Jim before they turned and started walking toward the front door. Just as they approached the door they turned as Jim said, "I feel very bad for you. You are good people. I will give the matter consideration and let you know if I change my mind."

Then Jim, Maggie and I sat down again to finish dinner. There was an eerie silence as nobody really knew what to say. I glanced over at Jim as he finished eating and he appeared to be deep in thought. In a few minutes, Jim looked up from his food and turned towards Maggie. "Thank you so much for inviting me. The food was delicious. Lonny, I'll be in touch."

Then he stood and walked out the front door.

Maggie glanced over at me. "Do you think he'll help Jack?"

"I don't think so but stranger things have happened. It's too bad he's getting sucked into this Heygood mess."

CHAPTER 13

Two weeks later Pete and I walked out of the Professional Building on Forest Lane after our fourth doctor's visit of the day. Previously, the results of the MRI pinpointed possible malignant tissue on Pete's prostrate. The subsequent MRI-guided biopsy confirmed the presence of cancer. Now, we had to determine the next steps.

Pete looked at me. "Son, I don't know what to do. Each of the doctors we talked to recommended a different treatment."

"I know, it's very confusing."

"All of the doctors recommended using their own machines. They said they had never heard of the other treatments."

"Well, they have millions of dollars tied up in their equipment and they need to pay it off. They're acting like businessmen."

"Don't doctors have to take some kind of oath? The hypocrite oath?"

I chuckled and shook my head. "No, Dad. That's

the Hippocratic Oath."

Pete stopped and shook his head. "Doctors never seemed to do things like that when I was younger. They did the best thing for their patients. You could trust them."

"Well, some of the treatments are new and there's not a long history of results so it may be years before the researchers can say which approach is best. So right now, everyone can recommend their own treatment."

Pete waved his arms. "Darn, it's just not fair. I'll be dead before they figure it out. What should I do?"

I couldn't think of anything uplifting to say so I provided a candid response—that was the best I could do. "Most of the treatments have possible significant side effects."

Pete took several more steps and stopped. "Yes, I know. Even though I don't have sex very often, I'd still like to be able to have it. What I am most afraid of is having to wear a diaper. If a man can't control his bowels or bladder then you have to wonder if life is worth living."

"I think what we have to do is find the least invasive treatment for you that will stop your cancer."

Pete turned and smiled. "Yes, sir."

I put my hand on Pete's shoulder. "We can't count on anybody to make the best decision for you. We are going to have to do some research on our own to learn more about all of these treatment options before we make a decision. Maybe we can talk to some doctors who don't have skin in the game who can give us unbiased advice."

"Thank you, son. I don't know what I'd do without you."

CHAPTER 14

For the first time in weeks, I left National Airlines on time and headed to Dallas on State Highway 183. The latest purchase agreement proposal for the acquisition of slots and routes from Global Airlines had been fashioned earlier in the day and reviewed by our legal department that afternoon. Skip Wise had taken the day off but wanted to see the agreement today. For security reasons, I decided to hand-deliver the document rather than email it.

Skip was born and bred in ritzy Highland Park and went to business school at SMU. Recently, he purchased a twelve-hundred-square-foot bungalow with a prestigious address for over one million dollars a few blocks from his parents' home. The price seemed astronomical but as Skip frequently said, "I had to go small to buy in."

Senior leadership considered Skip to be one of the bright young stars at National. He had been specially tracked for rapid advancement since his first year at the company. His recent promotion to vice president had come as a surprise to many. Some people thought that at the age of thirty Skip was not ready to assume the reigns of Corporate Development. I found Skip to be very likable, almost like a little brother, but now I reported to him on Project Green Field.

I turned off of Lovers Lane toward his bungalow—a small, one story, red brick house nestled on a large lot. Recently erected mansions surrounded Skip's home. Maybe this wasn't a bad investment after all—someone might buy his property just for the dirt. No parking spots were available in front so I turned the corner and found a parking spot. It was a short walk to Skip's home and I quickly rounded the corner on the sidewalk. Just then, I saw a striking, athletic-looking, black-haired woman emerge from Skip's front door. I laughed to myself that she was certainly a good reason to stay home from work. I didn't know if Skip had a girlfriend—we never discussed it—but this was certainly a pleasant surprise. When she reached the sidewalk she abruptly turned and started walking directly towards me. I would get a good look at her shortly. When we were within five feet of each other I smiled and said, "Hello, nice day."

She looked at me and her face showed no emotion. Her skinny legs and arms were long while her torso was short. We glanced at each other. She said nothing. Her steely blue eyes looked cold and her jet-black hair fell on her shoulders. She was very sexy but, in a way, almost looked scary—sort of like a black widow. Soon I reached Skip's front door which was slightly ajar. I heard Skip moaning in the other room.

I took one step inside and said, "Hello, Skip."

He spoke softly, as if he was out of breath. "Who is it?"

"It's Lonny. Did you just get lucky? Haha. Who was that stone-cold knockout that just left?"

"Ah."

"You certainly have upgraded!"

Then I walked into Skip's kitchen. He laid on the floor holding his face.

"Are you ok? Rough sex? Haha."

Skip winced and looked up. "No, she's just a friend."

Skip seemed dazed. I wondered if he was ok and so I leaned over and took a closer look. Abrasions and bruises were noticeable on his face and arms—he could have passed for a mugging victim. I stopped joking. "Skip, are you ok? What happened?"

"Ah...I fell down. Tripped over that damn rug."

Skip slowly rose to his feet, took a few shaky steps towards the kitchen table and sat down. I opened my briefcase and pulled out our latest purchase proposal. A trickle of blood flowed from his nose. I looked at Skip. "Would you like to go over this now?"

"Not really. Why don't we go over this tomorrow? I'm not up to it at the moment."

I nodded, closed my briefcase and started walking towards the front door. After taking a few steps, I turned to look back. "Skip, my friend, I'll catch you on the flip side."

Skip just nodded. What was I supposed to think? Skip's visitor now seemed shrouded in mystery and I wondered if she had anything to do with his current condition.

CHAPTER 15

Today was going to be the first round of negotiations between Assistant Attorney General Al Stephens and Jim Taggart around the compensation to be provided to Jack Heygood in exchange for his testimony in the retrial of William Clayton, the poster boy for white collar crime in the United States. I arrived in the lobby of the Dallas skyscraper that housed Jim's law firm. We planned to walk together over to the Earl Campbell Federal Building on Commerce Street for the negotiation.

Surprisingly, Jim Taggart seemed to be in an upbeat mood. He was shocked when Jack's son and sister confronted him at my house a few weeks earlier. But he had given their pleas to represent Jack consideration and, in the end, decided to negotiate for Jack. I wondered why Jim changed his mind. We were a block away from the Federal Building and I looked at Jim. "So, why are we here together to negotiate with the feds?"

Jim paused briefly as we waited for the light to change and we could cross the street. "Personally, I couldn't care less if Jack Heygood spends the next twenty years in prison. My only concern is for his son Mark. The kid has been through an awful lot with the murder of his mother and the incarceration of his father. I am doing this for the kid."

We walked another half a block and could see the main entrance to the Federal Building. Jim studied a couple of men engaged in an animated conversation on the sidewalk. "The tall, bald guy on the left is Al Stephens, Assistant Attorney General of the United States. The other guy is Sam Gilbert on the Texas Attorney General's staff in Austin."

"I saw Stephens on TV when they interviewed him in Atlanta after the Appeals Court announced their decision to overturn Clayton's conviction. Do you know them?"

"I have had dealings with both."

We walked up to the two men and Jim slapped Sam Gilbert on the back and extended his hand. Then he looked at Al Stephens. An awkward moment of silence followed before they shook hands. Al looked around and said, "Let's get going. I have to catch a plane to Hong Kong in a couple of hours."

Led by Al's three-man security detail, we walked in through the main entrance and found we were at the end of a very long line of people trying to go through security. Al took one long look at the line and pointed his security men to the left. "This is bullshit. Let's go."

We moved to the left and went in through the out door. The security alarms immediately went off as we moved forward. Al's security detail flashed their badges as we passed the checkpoint. The security guards glared at us. You could hear murmurings from the people waiting to go through the metal detector. We moved directly to the elevators and got off on the fourth floor. A large conference room paneled with wood had been reserved for the negotiation. Pictures of the United States Supreme Court Justices adorned the walls. Stephens and Gilbert sat directly across the table from Jim and me. Coffee arrived and we were ready to begin.

Stephens added a little sugar to his coffee and took a sip from his Dixie cup. "Frankly, I don't understand why we are here. The Appeals Court ruling was flawed. There was no prosecutorial misconduct."

Jim Taggart laughed. "Al, a competent, first-semester law student could enumerate the improprieties."

Al's face became red. "What?"

"Accept the ruling, it's a *fait accompli*."

"That's—"

Jim looked at his watch and interrupted, "You have to catch a plane to Hong Kong and I have senior executives from a distressed company cooling their heels in my office while the creditors are snarling at their doors. Can we please get on with it?"

Stephens sneered at Jim. "Taggart, I've hated your guts for the last twenty years ever since you handled the appeal for that scumbag Willie Drumingo. I hope you heard that Drumingo is getting paroled from prison next month. If he kills anyone else then it's all on you."

Jim momentarily looked down and his face became expressionless. "No, I didn't hear that. I don't like myself either. That wasn't my finest moment."

Al Stephens' mouth opened and he appeared completely surprised by the response but said nothing for several seconds and finally collected himself. "Gents, we want Heygood to testify at William Clayton's retrial. We are prepared to offer a fair and just settlement."

Gilbert briefly glanced at Stephens and then starred at us for a few moments. "Because of our close relationship with the Department of Justice, the State of Texas is prepared to guarantee that Heygood will be released when he first comes up for parole in three years."

Jim Taggart shook his head from side-to-side and remained silent.

Al Stephens' face turned a dark shade of red. Pausing for a moment, he growled at Taggart, "You're making a big mistake. This is the best deal you'll get. If you pass, I'll make sure Heygood never gets out."

Taggart smiled. "Heygood's testimony was instrumental in securing the convictions of all of the Tropical insiders. Without it, the best you could have done was a hung jury. Do you remember the interviews with the jurors after Clayton's trial ended? Your offer is not satisfactory."

Gilbert puffed up his cheeks. "Ok, ok, Heygood could walk off a prison farm within a year of his testifying. The guards would turn their backs and he could leave."

Taggart shook his head and grimaced. "The prison guards could shoot him in the back or the Texas Rangers could arrest him at any time. That's no solution."

Gilbert pounded his fist on the table. "That's our final offer. Heygood was convicted in a Texas court for shooting up a North Dallas neighborhood. The Governor ran on a law and order platform. He can't be linked to Heygood's early release. That's the best we can do."

Taggart looked directly at Al Stephens and countered, "William Clayton was on the front of *Time Magazine* as the symbol of white-collar crime. How is that going to play if the Federal Government has to release the Tropical kingpin because they can't put a case together?"

Stephens slammed his fist on the table. "Do you know who you are talking to? Taggart, you son of a bitch; just what do you propose?"

"The *quid pro quo* for his testimony against William Clayton is a full pardon from the Governor of Texas."

Stephens looked at Gilbert and nodded. Gilbert's mouth was open as he stared at Stephens. "I am not authorized to make this deal."

Stephens leaned back in his chair. "The Attorney General will call the Governor to discuss what needs to be done in the best interests of this great country."

CHAPTER 16

It was too cold of a night to be playing baseball. The wind blew from the north and the temperature was in the mid-forties. The 18U (ages eighteen and under) Dallas Generals had scheduled an exhibition game on a Tuesday night in December against the Arlington Braves at TCU. General Manager Mike Rizzo wanted to get the team together to play a game before Christmas and the beginning of the high school baseball season. Mike was the founder and manager of the Generals and a fixture in the Dallas select baseball scene as his teams had won numerous national championships and many former Generals were playing professional baseball. He was a former big-league player and a man of integrity who had become a successful businessman in Dallas after receiving his law degree from Harvard. His involvement in youth baseball was solely motivated by his love for the game.

Mike's business focused on the operational and

financial restructuring of distressed companies. As his business flourished and expanded outside of Texas to California, he was not able to spend as much time with the team as he had in previous seasons. But when he was in town he would always lead the practices and coach in the games. Mike now spends the majority of his time in California working out of his ocean-view home in the Pacific Palisades.

The Generals were an elite select team that recruited players from across the state of Texas. Most of the nucleus of last year's team that finished second in the prestigious National Championship Tournament (NCT) in Phoenix would be back. Joe and I drove over early from Dallas to avoid the rush-hour traffic and stopped to eat some tacos at a local restaurant chain on the south end of campus.

Joe and I sat at a counter that faced the window. I looked at Joe. "Who's coming back from last year's team? You guys came close at the NCT last summer. Maybe Mike will pick up some new kids to beef up the roster."

Joe poured hot sauce on his tacos and took a couple of bites. "I think the infield is intact. Mark Heygood is going to play 1st base. Juan Francisco is a lock for 2nd. Of course, Tyrone Alberts will play shortstop. Owen Sorensen will return at 3rd base and Brock Dillard will catch. The outfield is another story. Murray McClure and I will start but the big question is whether Josh Baker will return."

"Have you heard anything from Josh recently?"

"We've talked a couple of times. He says he wants to stay with us again at the house if he plays. His high school team is still in the football playoffs so he will not be coming in from Lubbock for the scrimmage tonight."

I took a long drink of my iced tea. "If he decides to take a football ride then he'll probably have to report to college in June for summer school."

Joe picked up his fourth taco and took a bite. "I bet if he plays he will just be with us until the MLB draft in June. He really wants to sign."

I got a refill on my iced tea before we walked out to the car. The stadium was three blocks to the west and the lights were already on. Our short drive over took a couple of minutes and the stadium lot was almost vacant so we parked twenty feet away from the walkway into the stadium down the left field line. A few players had already arrived and were stretching on the field. Joe walked down to the field and dropped his bag in the dugout on the 1st base side. Only a handful of parents were in the stands—it was too cold to sit on aluminum bleachers for three hours.

Thirty minutes later we were ready to start. Two college coaches walked into the stadium and sat next to each other ten rows up directly behind home plate. Each carried a radar gun to track the speed of the pitches. Hopefully, Joe would have a good showing. Most of the other kids on the Generals had committed to colleges after sifting through multiple opportunities but Joe had not received any offers yet. I moved to my left and got a good glimpse of the college scouts. Buddy Johnson, the assistant coach and recruiting coordinator for Our Savior's University (OSU), pulled out his radar gun. He was a huge man that reminded me of a bear. I briefly met him last summer. His hands were like bear paws that totally engulfed you when you shook hands. Buddy was OSU's top scout and a fixture at select baseball games in the Dallas area throughout the summer. No one outworked him. At one time, Joe had hoped to get an offer from Buddy but nothing materialized. The other coach, Chip Studstill, an up-and-coming assistant at a state school who coached pitching when not recruiting, opened a notebook.

Since this was an exhibition game, all of the players would bat. Joe would start on the bench, pitch in the third inning and then move to the outfield for the remainder of the game. I sat anxiously in my seat through the first inning waiting for Joe's first plate appearance. I looked over at the two college scouts. The scrimmage did not seem to have their full attention as they engaged in a lively conversation. Joe was on deck when the Generals recorded their third out so he would lead off in the next inning. Since Joe was not playing in the field I took a break and walked around the adjacent running track to relieve the tension.

When I returned to the baseball field Joe was in the batter's box awaiting his first pitch. Fortunately, I hadn't missed any of the action. The pitcher got the signal from the catcher and went into his wind-up. The ball left his hand and headed towards the plate. Joe turned and his bat squarely hit the ball which exploded off the bat and headed to right field. The outfielder didn't move as the ball sailed over the fence and onto the berm behind it. I watched Joe start to circle the bases but as he reached second I glanced over at the two scouts. Their heads were down and took copious notes. Maybe that was a good sign?

Midway through the second inning Joe and one of the catchers went down to the bullpen to warm up. The next inning would be Joe's opportunity to showcase his talents on the mound. Finally, the second inning ended and Joe trotted out to the mound. After ten warm-up pitches, the leadoff batter got set in the batter's box. A radar gun was attached to the rail behind home and the pitch speeds were displayed on the corner of the scoreboard. The batter watched a 92-mph fastball on the corner of the plate for a strike. The second pitch came down the middle of the plate at 93 mph. The batter swung late and missed the ball. Joe looked in to the catcher for the signal, became set and threw the ball towards home. The batter swung and missed as he was fooled by a change-up at 72 mph.

Joe's second batter dug into the batter's box. As Joe released his first pitch, the batter turned and squared up to bunt the ball. The ball jumped off the bat towards first base and rolled six feet before it stopped. Since Joe was left-handed his momentum pulled him towards third base after he released the ball; however, he was quick enough to stop, run to the ball and throw it to Mark Heygood playing first base. The throw beat the batter to the base by a step so there were two outs. The next batter had received plenty of attention from the scouts. He would be a more formidable challenge than the first two batters. Joe wound up and threw a twelve-six curve ball that surprised the batter for strike one. The second pitch was fouled straight back over the backstop for strike two. The catcher gave his signal and Joe began his pitching motion. The pitch headed straight at the batter who stiffened anticipating impact but the pitch curved away from him and over the plate for strike three. Nice outing! I glanced at the scouts. Their heads were down and they were writing notes. Buddy got up and walked towards the mezzanine.

After he left, Chip Studstill pulled out his cell phone and started talking.

I noticed that Mike Rizzo left the Generals' dugout and sat in the stands and while talking on his phone. Game management had been left in capable hands of Head Coach Ronny Espinosa and Assistant Coach Stan White who had guided the Generals to a second-place finish in the NCT last summer in Phoenix. Coach Ronny is thirty-six years old and was born and bred in California's Central Valley. Ronny's parents were migrant farm workers who eventually settled in Bakersfield, California. He stands a little under 5'10" with dark skin and a pencil-thin mustache. Coach Ronny earned all-conference honors as a second baseman at a small, Division II college in California and later played for three years in the Mexican League. He was never able to break into the minor leagues because of his below-average hitting skills. Rumors abounded last season about Ronny's suspected dalliances with a player's mother. I spotted him in a compromising position late at night in a hotel swimming pool during a tournament in Atlanta. Coach Stan is six feet tall and probably weighs around 200 pounds. He was a junior college All-American and played four years in the Dodgers organization, advancing to AA before being released. Last season he was suckered into a scam orchestrated by one of the parents on the team and lost a sizeable amount of money. Both Ronny and Stan have coached select baseball teams in Dallas for several summers.

The temperature dropped as the northern breeze swept through the stadium. The game couldn't end soon enough as my teeth chattered and Joe had school in the morning. As the Generals left the dugout, Mike Rizzo motioned Joe and me over. Mike looked at Joe and smiled. "I think you impressed some coaches tonight. Both Chip Studstill and Buddy Johnson wanted your cell phone number so expect a call when you're driving back to Dallas."

Joe smiled. "Thanks Mr. Rizzo, I'll let you know what they say."

Mike Rizzo looked me in the eyes. "Sorry that Mark Heygood couldn't make it tonight."

"I know. He's living with his aunt and finishing high school in Oklahoma City. It's too far to travel on a school night. But he'll be living with Joe and me again next summer during baseball season."

"He's had a tough life. I called a few coaches to talk him up."

"Thanks. His family appreciates it."

Mike raised his eyebrows and his mouth flattened. "He's on a number of backup recruiting lists—he may get a scholarship if the preferred recruits go elsewhere."

"I hope his baseball career doesn't end this summer."

"Me too. I'll keep working on it." Then Mike turned and started to walk back to the dugout.

Joe and I got in the car and turned on the heat full blast before we started the forty-mile drive home to Dallas. Then Joe's phone started to ring. He picked up the call and looked at over at me. "Hi Coach Johnson, thank you very much."

There was a moment of silence as Joe listened to Buddy Johnson.

"Coach, thank you very much. Yes, I am very interested in playing for you."

Joe listened to Buddy for three more minutes.

"Yes, I will apply online and have my SAT scores

sent to Admissions...Thanks again."

Joe hung up his phone and turned to me. "Dad, Buddy thinks he will be able to get me a scholarship to OSU."

"That's great. It's nice to get a little love from the coaches."

We made our way north on University towards Interstate 30 just ahead. I stopped at the intersection and made a right turn to get east bound on the Interstate. Then Joe's phone started to ring again. Joe picked up. "Hi Coach Studstill...Thank you very much...Yes, I am very interested in visiting your campus... Thanks again."

Joe Hung up his phone just as we passed Oakland Blvd and I looked over. "Well, what did he say?"

"Coach Studstill wants us to visit campus."

"Did he say anything else?"

"Yeah, he says he has scholarship money for me."

Finally, Joe's fortunes had changed. He might be playing college baseball after all.

CHAPTER 17

We planned to meet at the Screwball Sports Bar in very far North Dallas just south of the Sam Rayburn Tollway. I was the first to arrive and sat down at the oval-shaped bar. Eight TVs hung from the ceiling inside of the bar. Twenty-five tables were behind the bar opposite to the front entrance—half were square while the others were circular. Twelve TVs lined the side and back walls. Most of the patrons looked like they had just stepped off the golf course—still wearing their golf hats with sun glasses perched on top. The wait staff consisted of fifteen gorgeous, hard-bodied, scantily-clad, young ladies. Their tops were very revealing and showcased the ladies' ample cleavage while the bottoms covered just a little bit more than a G string. I understood why Jack Heygood picked this place to meet Jim Taggart and myself.

Jack arrived next and had a wide grin on his face. We shook hands and Jack settled onto an adjacent bar stool. His prosthetic left forearm and hand were barely noticeable under his long sleeve. Jack ordered an IPA, took a sip and turned to me. "It's great to be out. I knew Taggart could get it done."

"Why were you so sure Jim would be successful?"

Jack leaned back and laughed. "He kicked Al Stephens' ass twenty years ago during the Drumingo appeal. He had the psychological edge. Stephens is still licking his wounds from that encounter. I knew Jim's presence would distract him and cause him to focus on the past."

I took a couple of sips of my beer. "Stephens came pretty close to losing it a couple of times during the negotiation with Jim."

"Haha, that's great! The reversal of Clayton's conviction drove him to the edge so I knew it wouldn't take much to push him over."

I looked around and took in the sights. "Well, I can see why you picked this place to meet with us."

Jack laughed. "I didn't come here for the chicks. I came for the sashimi...But the view is nice! Last year, when I came to Dallas to get money and watch Mark play baseball I basically lived here. A couple of the girls even asked me to shack up when I visited."

Jack's boastful manner didn't surprise me but I didn't want to listen. I gazed down at my watch. "Taggart is late—I wonder what's holding him up. By the way, why did you want to meet with us?"

"You might be surprised, but I wanted to buy you guys some lunch to thank you for getting me out of prison...and tell you about my next business venture. Do you think Taggart blew us off?"

"Taggart is a man of his word and will be here."

We ordered a couple of more beers and watched a little of the basketball game on the nearest TV. Just then Jim Taggart walked in the front entrance of the Screwball. He carried a folder and walked over to us. After we exchanged pleasantries, Jack suggested we move to a table in the back where we could talk. Jack sat to my left while Taggart sat across the table. After ordering another round of beers. Jack turned to Jim. "You know I really appreciate your helping me out. I'll never forget your pro bono work."

Taggart looked at Jack and laughed. "What do you mean pro bono work?"

Jack gulped. "You know, getting me out."

Jim studied Jack for several seconds. "I don't do pro bono work for felons anymore."

Jack's mouth dropped. Jim opened his folder and handed Jack a piece of paper. "That's your bill for legal services rendered."

His eyes widened as he glanced at the paper for a couple of minutes and then looked up. "One hundred thousand dollars is a lot of money!"

"Not really. I got your ass out of the state prison. Next time, before you send your sister and son to beg for legal services, you might want to tell them they should ask what it will cost."

Jack shook his head. "Ok, ok, I pay my debts. You'll get your money...but I want to tell you about a business opportunity...maybe it would be beneficial for you to take an equity stake instead?"

Taggart leaned back in his chair and his face was expressionless. "Jack, I want my one-hundred thousand dollars but since I am here and you are buying lunch I'll stay and listen to your spiel."

A beautiful waitress walked over to the table

and stood between Jack and me. She stood 5'8" with black hair and brown eyes and a tight figure that looked like it was ready to bust out of her scanty but pleasing outfit. Jack immediately put his arm around her waist and leaned in so his head touched her breast. She winked at Jack and smiled at Jim and me. "What can I get you gentlemen to eat?"

Jack ordered first. "Give me the Tuna Takata sashimi and two street tacos."

Jim quickly turned the pages of the menu. "I'll have the Big Tuna Tower."

Nothing really jumped out at me on the menu but I didn't want to hold things up. "The Flaming Volcano Rolls would be nice, thanks."

The waitress smiled and headed to the kitchen.

I noticed that Jack stared at a manager who stood inside the oval bar. His hair was slicked back and he had a tattoo on his arm. "I know that guy, I've seen him before."

"Where have you seen him?" I asked.

After several seconds, Jack leaned back and laughed. "Oh yeah, now I know. I can't believe it. He was the star of the porno movie I watched last night."

Taggart and I exchanged glances. Taggart shook his head. "Jack, I would have thought your stay in prison would have invited some introspection."

With a big grin on his face, Jack held up both of his hands. He was totally unrepentant.

In a few minutes the food finally arrived and we dug in. Jack shoveled down the street tacos as I looked over. "So, Jack, tell us about your business opportunity."

Still holding his taco, Jack looked up. "Green gold."

"Huh, what do you mean, green gold?"

"In six weeks, I'm going to make a presentation to some venture capitalists to get funding. I need one million dollars of start-up money."

I shook my head. "So what is your business concept?"

Jack paused for a few moments and ate some of the sashimi. "I have options to buy all of the production from three-hundred and fifty acres of land in Mexico—the Michoacán State, high up, on the sides of old volcanos. Perfect for growing avocados year around. The avocado market is skyrocketing."

"You know, they mentioned that on a news program I watched a few months ago," I added. "Well, what about organized crime, is it safe down there?"

"Another business partner can pull together a team of former Mexican Army soldiers that can provide security."

"What about logistics?"

"We plan for all of our production to flow to the United States and have access to distribution facilities in Michoacán and Dallas off of Loop 12. Grocery store chains in Texas are more than happy to purchase all of our production."

"Can you pull this off?" I asked.

Jack laughed and looked at Jim and me. "This is a slam dunk. Once we get the operation underway with the initial funding, we expect the investors will provide another round of capital, probably fifteen to twenty million dollars."

I noticed there were two men sitting at the oval bar glancing over at us. They would look away and then always come back to focus on us. One was bald with a smirk on his face and chewing gum while the other was shorter and stockier with thick jet-black hair.

Jack looked over at Taggart. "Jim you've just been heads-down eating food and haven't said anything. What are your thoughts?"

Jim held a sushi roll and looked up. "Your proposal appears to have a modicum of legitimacy buried somewhere in it."

I burst out laughing.

Jack's face tightened up. "Wait a minute; all is good. Trust me."

Taggart glared at Jack and then briefly paused. "A very smart businessman from Forney, Texas once told me that if a deal looks too good to be true then it probably is. Jack, with your track record, you need to put some points on the scoreboard before I will take you seriously."

I nodded in agreement. Jack looked around. "Guys, I want you to be my partners. I can offer you an equity position. Each of you has unique skills that could benefit my operation."

Lunch was over. We got up to leave and made our way outside into the bright sunshine. It took me a few seconds for my eyes to adjust to the brightness. Just as we reached our cars, I glanced to my left and saw the two men that were sitting at the bar and staring at us. The taller man still had a smirk on his face and was chewing gum. Then in an instant he pulled out a shotgun, aimed at us and fired. We all hit the deck and hugged the asphalt.

Taggart looked over at Jack and screamed, "What now, Jack?

Jack shook his head in disbelief and the hair on top of his head moved. I chuckled, "Jesus Christ, is that a rug on your head?"

Taggart and I started laughing and the two men across the parking lot looked at us in bewilderment. Then the taller man pumped his shotgun and fired again. The pellets flew a few feet over our heads. A police car siren could be heard in the distance so the two men fled and headed at a high speed towards the Dallas North Tollway.

Jack got up and dusted himself off. "They were trying to kill me!"

Taggart laughed. "No, that was only a warning. If they wanted to kill you we would be scraping you up from the parking lot."

As Taggart got into his car, he turned to Jack, smiled and said, "Maybe I might want to wait before I take my equity stake."

Jack and I stood there in the middle of the parking lot and then he turned to me. "What do you think?"

I looked at Jack and grimaced. "Well, I have been having some problems of my own. Those guys may have been shooting at me."

Jack looked at me in disbelief and walked to his car.

CHAPTER 18

The warm breeze from the south felt refreshing as I tried to unwind on my patio after the shooting in the Screwball parking lot. Three empty Coors cans sat on the table. Hearing someone try to lift the latch on the fence gate that leads to the front yard, I glanced to my left. What was happening? Who was there? Fortunately, the latch wouldn't move—the gate was locked. Then I heard three knocks. "Hey Lonny, are you back here?"

I immediately recognized the voice of Lieutenant Vince Truex of the Dallas Police Department. I got up to open the gate. "C'mon in Vince."

Vince walked over to the patio table and sat down directly across from me. He looked at me quizzically. "Well, aren't you going to offer me a beer?"

I reached down into the twelve-pack, grabbed a beer and handed it to Vince. Soon, I heard a pop and Vince took a large gulp. "I heard you were involved in a shootout in the parking lot of a strip club in far North Dallas."

I smiled. "That's not completely accurate, it was a sports bar but the waitresses didn't leave much to the imagination."

Vince shook his head. "Ok, tell me what happened."

"I had just finished lunch with Jack Heygood and Jim Taggart. We were standing in the parking lot talking. I heard the sound of someone racking a shotgun and looked over. The next thing I knew shot gun pellets were flying over my head."

"Why did you and Taggart meet Heygood for lunch?"

"Heygood wanted to tell us about his latest scheme—an avocado business in Mexico. Taggart wanted to collect his legal fee for negotiating Jack's release from prison. I didn't have anything on my calendar and a free lunch at the Screwball definitely had some allure."

Vince rolled his eyes. "You and Taggart are making a huge mistake hanging around with Heygood. He's bad news and everyone around him usually ends up taking the gaff. So tell me about the shooting."

"While we were eating I noticed a couple of guys sitting at the bar that were staring at us. Whenever I looked at them they turned and looked in another direction. The taller bald man shot the gun at us. The short, stocky guy just watched."

"So why would they shoot at you?"

I grabbed another beer from the twelve pack. "I am not sure of their target. Jack Heygood has a list of enemies a mile long from his days at Tropical Investments. He's trying get involved in a business in Mexico. Maybe someone doesn't want him to be a player. With Jack there are lots of possibilities"

"Yeah, he might be stepping on the toes of organized crime or bringing unwanted publicity," added Vince.

I took another sip of beer. "Another thing, you remember the guys that Dad found in the house? If Veritas Associates is involved to find and plug a leak at National Airlines then anything is possible."

"Yeah, both you and Heygood could be hot." Vince laughed and continued, "Don't invite me to lunch with you guys anytime soon."

Vince took another drink of beer. "Seriously, are you carrying? You need to be ready because you might not have time to get ready."

"Good point, I need to keep my Glock with me."

Vince leaned back in his chair and paused for a moment. "So, getting back to Veritas Associates, what's happening with your secret project?"

"We are still negotiating with our acquisition target."

Truex shook his head knowingly. "Do you guys think that sensitive information about the negotiation is still being passed to your competitor?"

"The senior leaders haven't mentioned that lately."

Vince adjusted himself in his chair. "Is anything else out of the ordinary happening at National Airlines?"

"Well, Skip Wise, my partner on the negotiating team seems to have lost it?"

"After I told him about Dad getting beat up and what you said about Veritas Associates, he became paranoid and thinks that Veritas could come after him."

"Really? I wonder why?"

"Well, something else, I went to his bungalow in Highland Park a few weeks ago and saw this mysterious woman exit. She was beautiful with a dark complexion and long arms and legs—she reminded me of a black widow. When I walked in Skip was lying on the floor and his face was bleeding."

Vince grimaced. "That doesn't sound right."

"Skip didn't want to talk about it and sounded afraid."

"Maybe this is all related. Why don't we drive over and talk to Skip now?" suggested Vince Truex.

CHAPTER 19

Skip's bungalow was completely dark when Vince and I pulled up and parked in front. This trip could be a waste of time since there was no sign of Skip.

I turned to Vince. "He didn't answer his phone when I called but he hasn't been answering his phone lately."

Vince looked at the bungalow briefly and then turned to me. "Is Skip a close friend?"

"Not really, more of a business associate. We go out to lunch but I typically don't see him outside of work."

"Is he a peer?"

"No, not really. Skip is fifteen years younger than I and seems like a little brother but he is a VP and I report to him on the acquisition project."

"He seems sort of young for a VP."

"Yeah, he rose rapidly through the ranks."

"Was he ready?"

"Not really, he says the right things in meetings

but can be immature and sometimes has a superficial knowledge of the operation. One of the senior guys pulled me aside one day and told me I needed to keep Skip out of trouble."

"I wonder if he is experiencing more stress than he can't handle now."

"Good question. Well, since we're here, should we pound on the door?" I asked.

Vince nodded his head affirmatively. "Why not, let's do it."

Vince and I walked up the curved sidewalk to the front door. The doorbell was mounted on the wrong side of the door. I pushed it three times. We waited for a couple of minutes and there was no response.

Vince turned to leave. "Let's go. We'll catch him another time."

Then we heard a noise and the door opened a crack. Someone was home. "What do you want?"

It was Skip. "Como esta? It's Lonny."

"Who else is out there?

"My friend, Vince Truex, from the Dallas Police."

"What? What the hell are you doing here?"

Vince stepped forward. "Mr. Wise, I am with the Dallas Police and investigating the assault of Pete Jones. Can I talk to you?"

"Jesus Christ! Ok, ok come in," said Skip as he opened the door.

Vince and I walked in and Skip turned on the lights. He wore only his BVDs and motioned us into the kitchen. We all sat down around the kitchen table. Skip had black circles under his eyes and looked like he had been to hell and back.

I glanced at Vince and then back at Skip. "Skip, Skip, you're not looking good, guy."

"I'm ok, really," said Skip as he rested his elbow on the table.

"I wanted to tell you that someone took a couple of shots at Jack Heygood and me after lunch today."

Skip's left eye started to twitch. "Oh my God, was it those guys from Veritas Associates?"

"We don't know. They fled before the police arrived."

Vince pulled out his note pad from his pocket and looked at Skip.

"Mr. Wise, may I call you Skip?"

"Sure, sure. Whatever."

"Lonny mentioned that he saw a tall woman with black hair leaving your apartment before he found you bleeding on the kitchen floor."

Skip's eyes blinked several times and he fidgeted in his chair. "So what?"

Vince studied Skip for a few moments and squinted his eyes. "Who is she?"

Skip laughed. "I don't know…she never told me her name."

Truex made some notes in his book and then looked up. "So she was in your house and you didn't know her name?"

"Yeah, that's true," said Skip as he raised his hands slightly above the table.

"How could that be?" said Truex in disbelief.

"Haha. Well, let's just refer to her as the Black Widow like Lonny does. I met her over at Pedro's."

"The Mexican restaurant at the north end of Snyder Plaza?"

"Yeah."

Vince paused and took more notes. "So how did she end up in your house?"

"I had a bad week and was drinking at the bar

during happy hour. The margaritas with a little sangria blended in are outstanding. It's hard to stop at just one."

"What happened?"

"Well, the Black Widow sat down on the stool next to me and we started to talk. Soon she had her arm around me and played with my hair. She was hot. She was smoking hot."

Truex and I exchanged knowing glances as both of us had been there before in our younger days.

Vince looked at Skip. "Then what?"

"Her hand moved down on the top of my thigh. Then it moved to the inside of my thigh."

"What did you think?" I asked.

"Hell, I drank four margaritas and barely remembered my name. My face was numb. There was a buzz in my head. What was I supposed to think?"

The story amused me and I laughed. Then Skip's eyes widened and he continued, "The Black Widow said she wanted me."

"So you took her home?"

Skip raised his eye brows and smirked. "I don't have talent like that asking me for sex every day. Geez. What do you think I did?"

"So, what happened at your house?" inquired Lt. Truex.

"She wanted kinky sex and got on top of me. One thing led to another. It was crazy. We did lots of things I wouldn't want anyone to know about."

Skip shrugged his shoulders and added, "Then she left."

Truex continued to take copious notes. "When did you see her again?"

"The next day when she came back with the

pictures. She must have rigged up a camera."

"Pictures?" asked Vince.

Skip stood up. "I've told you too much. We're done."

"Ok, that's fine, Skip. Thank you for your cooperation."

Truex and I got up from the table and walked out of Skip's house and down the sidewalk to his car at the curb. Then he started the car and we headed back to my house. I looked over at Vince as we turned off of Lovers Lane onto Inwood Road. "Skip could be in some real trouble."

Vince nodded his head in agreement. "Maybe all the pieces will fit together."

CHAPTER 20

Sunday afternoon was beautiful. Maggie and I headed to the mall to return some Christmas clothing presents that didn't fit. Fortunately, I found an open parking space directly in front of the store we planned to visit. Before I could unfasten my seatbelt I felt Maggie's hand on my arm. "Lonny, could we talk for a few moments before we go in?"

"Sure, that's fine."

"I have been thinking about some of things Joan said when she yelled in the front yard."

Her remark caught me surprise and I wondered what it was leading to. "What do you mean by that?"

"Well...she said we are not right for each other."

What should I think about Maggie's comments? One thing was clear—Joan was the gift that keeps on giving. I began to get angry but tried to relax and not start yelling.

I turned to Maggie. "Put that in context, Joan just got dumped by her boyfriend and panicked.

Don't give her comments a second thought."

Maggie shrugged her shoulders. "Lonny, it's not that easy."

I turned and hugged her. "You'll be fine."

Maggie held my hand and then we embraced. Hopefully, Maggie and I could put the latest mess with Joan behind us.

We exited the *Bullitt* and headed into the mall. Fortunately, the crowd was pretty sparse and there were only four people in front of us in the return line. Then I heard a familiar voice and glanced to my left. There was Jack Heygood, his arm around a blonde woman wearing sunglasses. The woman wore a black nylon tee shirt with two lines of script, silver lettering on the front that said, "*Money Talk, Bullshit Walk.*" The kind of tacky shirt you would expect to see on the discount rack at a truck stop. I had not heard from Jack since our ill-fated lunch at the Screwball with Jim Taggart a month ago. He saw me and headed in our direction. "Well hello, Lonny. Long time no see," said Jack as he slapped me on the back.

I nodded and extended my hand. "Jack, do you know Maggie?"

"I don't believe that I've had the pleasure."

I glanced at the woman with Jack. Her big sunglasses covered a large part of her face. "How are you doing?"

"Something close to nothing," she responded.

Her awkward response caught me by surprise. So I paused for a moment. "I'm Lonny Jones and this is Maggie, my fiancée."

"So that's what you call yourself in Dallas?"

Maggie glanced at the blonde and had a puzzled look on her face. The blonde smiled at Maggie and then looked at me. "You called yourself Jimmy Woodcock when we took a shower together in Delray Beach last summer. That's all you got for your two hundred dollars."

Oh my God, it was Sunny. I was speechless. Sunny took off her sunglasses and winked at me.

Jack chuckled. "Sunny be nice...let bygones be bygones."

The smile left Sunny's face. "Yeah right," Sunny said as she cocked her head backwards.

Maggie let go of my hand, abruptly turned and started walking away.

Jack shook his head. "Look, Lonny, I am really sorry about this. I'm sure Maggie will understand when she cools down. She'll probably laugh about it."

A smile appeared on Sunny's face. "Jimmy, payback is a bitch. By the way, I knew your name was bogus after I got one look at you in the shower."

Sunny's combination of cheap shots left me reeling and I wasn't sure what was going to come out of her mouth next. I turned and immediately started looking for Maggie. How could I get out of the dog house?

Then I heard Sunny's voice and looked back at Jack and her. Sunny held her head at an angle and said, "Go get her. Don't let opportunity boogie."

● ● ●

I caught up with Maggie an hour later at the other end of the mall. Her face was red and she looked like she had been crying. "Maggie, I can explain."

Maggie didn't respond and remained silent as we walked to the car. Once inside all hell broke loose.

Maggie got in my face. "I have never been so humiliated in my life. How could you do that to me?"

I raised my hands and shook my head. "Ah–"

"Did you take a shower with that woman?"

"Well, actually not, we never quite made it into the shower."

As soon as those words got out of my mouth I realized that they might not be helpful.

"Ahhh," said Maggie as she started to cry.

"It's not what you think. I visited Florida when Jack was on the run. Truex and I were looking for him. I had an opportunity to go to Delray Beach and took it. I've told you that before."

"You never told me that you got naked with that woman."

"It just happened. I needed to keep her in the apartment until Jack arrived."

"I bet you enjoyed that! So you cheated on me with a prostitute?"

That remark hit a nerve and I wasn't going to let it go unanswered. "Whatever I did, it wasn't cheating. Don't you remember? You left me and moved to Houston to be with your daughters."

"I can't believe you are throwing that in my face! I was true to you!"

We stopped talking for a minute and looked at each other. A tear trickled down her face. "Lonny, I don't know you! I think we need to spend some time apart. I'm moving out."

We drove back to my house in silence. Neither one of us wanted to talk. As soon as we pulled up in the driveway, Maggie jumped out and headed to the bedroom. In minutes her suitcases were open on the bed and clothes were being thrown in. I decided to leave her alone to cool down and not pursue any additional discussions at this point. Shortly, Maggie walked through the living room and stopped at the front door. Then she turned and looked at me. "I think my leaving is for the best. I don't think we can make it."

I was stunned and breathing hard. What could I say? "Maggie, let's talk about this?"

Maggie stared at me for a moment and her eyes narrowed. "No, my mind is made up."

Then I watched the love of my life walk down the sidewalk to her Jeep Cherokee and drive away. I felt the same empty feeling as I did last summer when Maggie announced that she was leaving me and moving to Houston to be closer to her daughters and grandchildren. We managed to survive that episode and get back together, but this time, I wasn't sure.

CHAPTER 21

Jack and I waited in the conference room at Simi Valley Combinator (SVC), a firm that specialized in working with start-ups with offices northwest of Los Angeles. SVC helped start-ups to best articulate their business model and value proposition to increase the likelihood of funding. Unlike many of the similar firms in the Bay Area, SVC was not limited to technology-focused opportunities. Many start-ups applied to work with SVC but only a few were selected. Jack had relocated to Los Angeles to refine his proposal at SVC. In addition, he had engaged the services of a couple of starving graduate students on the cheap to do some analytics in the cloud. Now it was time for Demo Day where the selected start-ups were each given thirty minutes to present to a group of venture capitalists and angel investors and make their pitch for funding. Jack had offered to pay for my travel expenses and I had a lot of free time on my hands after Maggie moved out so

I came out here on a lark. Start-ups and venture capital had always intrigued me.

Jack was scheduled to be the second presenter of the day. He sat a couple of seats away and was deeply immersed in his slide deck. I got a cup of coffee and started reading the Los Angeles paper. Soon a door opened. A lady entered and walked over to Jack. "Mr. Heygood, you're up. The presentation will start in five minutes so let's go in and get you set up."

We got up and walked into the Demo Day presentation room. A large projection screen hung from the ceiling and a raised podium stood to the left. I moved to a seat in the back of the room while Jack stood at the podium and fired up his presentation. One of the venture capitalists left his program in the back row so I picked it up and turned the pages. The third page listed the venture capitalists and angel investors in attendance: Pete Stubbs and Tim Jett of Pine Tree Capital, Billy Jack Kimball and Laura Newell from Blacklock Partners, Vic Moskowicz from Blue Ridge Partners and several people I had never heard of.

The audience quieted down and Jack began his presentation. "Thank you for—"

Before Jack could get out another word, Laura Newell stood up and glared at Jack. Her comely looks and slim figure caught the attention of most of the men in the room. She was a brunette that stood 5'7' and probably weighed around one-hundred and twenty pounds. Her face was red and her nostrils flared as she gave Jack a riveting stare. "Mr. Heygood, I don't want to waste this esteemed group's time to listen to your tawdry proposal. Is this just some scam you cooked up with the other jailbirds while you were incarcerated?"

Pete Stubbs sat in the front row and turned back to look at Laura. "Laura, let's start with a touch of civility." Then he turned to Jack. "Mr. Heygood, your checkered past is of grave concern to us. We are giving you thirty minutes of our time because of the notable success you enjoyed raising capital for Tropical Investments and your feel for market opportunities."

Jack paused and pulled out an official-looking document from his brief case. Then he raised it to make it visible to everyone in the room. "This is the pardon I received from the Governor of Texas. He wouldn't have pardoned me if I weren't wrongly convicted and innocent of all charges. You know his reputation. I have been completely exonerated."

The room erupted and soon there were fifteen simultaneous conversations. Pete Stubbs stood up to bring order to the proceedings. Pete looked at the other investors. "Can we please proceed?"

All of the investors except Laura nodded their heads affirmatively. Jack clicked on the projector controls and his presentation appeared on the screen behind him. From his vast prior marketing experience, Jack knew that he wanted the investors to focus on him and that the presentation only served to reinforce his comments.

"I am going to present a business opportunity that will exploit the burgeoning demand for a commodity. Our economic research forecasts double-digit annual growth in demand for the foreseeable future. Our business model is uniquely designed to capture a large premium market share with the capability to scale rapidly and with efficiency."

Jack advanced the presentation beyond the title

slide. The next slide displayed a picture of a bowl full of guacamole followed by a slide with a picture of an avocado. He panned the room from the podium. "What is the global opportunity?"

A slide showing "6.1 Million Metric Tons" appeared next. Jack smiled in full sales mode.

Laura Newell raised her hand and stood. "Why should we have any confidence in your market size and share forecasts? Was there any science behind them or just some wild-ass guesses?"

Jack smiled as he looked directly at Laura. "Excellent question. Our forecast was based on cutting edge analytics. We considered historical trend and multiple explanatory variables."

Laura had a puzzled look on her face. "What? Could you provide more details?"

"Initially, we considered classical time series models. Then we moved on to also include explanatory variables such as the date of the Super Bowl and Cinco de Mayo when guacamole consumption soars. Neural network models provided the lowest forecast error…Next question."

Billy Jack Kimball raised his hand. "Are you a one-man band or do you have a team that could actually implement your proposal?"

"Thank you…That leads into my next slide." Jack advanced the presentation and continued. I like to think of my team as a group of all-stars—sort of my secret sauce—that will initially provide support and leadership on a consultative basis. Long term, I anticipate they will be full time members of the team."

The projected slide listed Jack's associates in Michoacán, Mexico—starting with Jorge Tatis, Jr.— whom I had never heard of before. Then Jack advanced to his next slide that displayed his key team members in the United States. I couldn't believe what I saw.

Jack continued, "Jim Taggart is the leading mergers and acquisition lawyer in Dallas with a national reputation–"

Laura Newell blurted out, "I know Jim. He's a good pick for you because he is also an expert at leading distressed companies through the bankruptcy process."

A brief outburst of laughter ensued. Jack did not appear fazed and, after a momentary pause, he turned and pointed at me. I knew what was coming next.

"Lonny Jones, sitting in the back row, is a transportation industry financial wizard."

This was all news to me and I now realized why Jack had invited me to Demo Day.

Jack continued, "Jerry Huggins is an expert in logistics and warehouse management in the North Texas area."

I shook my head in disbelief. Jerry Huggins had a past with Jack and a history of shenanigans. He was a horse's ass and a serial liar...but a fun guy to drink a beer with.

Vic Moskowicz from Blue Ridge Partners, sitting towards the back of the room, raised his hand and then stood to ask a question. "Mr. Heygood, you have tried to cultivate the appearance of your business plan being in motion. Have you actually started to execute your plan or are you just a PowerPoint cowboy?"

Jack raised his right hand and pointed his index finger toward the ceiling. "Very much the former. I have secured options to lease refrigerated storage facilities in Mexico and in Dallas. My representative in Mexico has purchased options to buy virtually unlimited avocado production at industry-low prices from some of the largest farms. Next week, I will firm up an agreement to lease a fleet of refrigerated semi-trailer trucks."

Vic gave an approving nod. We were nearing the end of the thirty-minute time slot with the investors so Jack quickly advanced the presentation to the next slide entitled "The Ask." The body of the slide contained one bullet: "$1,000,000 to conduct a Proof of Concept for a 10% equity stake."

Jack scanned the crowd of investors. "Once the POC is complete and proven to be successful, I anticipate requesting at least one additional round of funding."

Then the SVC program moderator stood. "This concludes Mr. Heygood's presentation. Our next presentation will begin in fifteen minutes. Thank you."

Jack had gathered his material and stepped down from the podium as several investors circled him to ask follow-on questions.

● ● ●

Thirty minutes later we're driving down Interstate 405 towards the Los Angeles International Airport. Jack had been silent so far and appeared to be deep in thought. Then I asked, "Well, do you think you'll get the initial funding?"

"Yes, of course. The only question is how much second-round funding I should ask for and how much of an equity stake will I need to give."

Jack looked over and smiled. He never suffered

from a lack of confidence.

"One thing surprised me in your presentation."

"What?"

"Laura Newell came after you at every opportunity. Do you have a past with her?"

"Haha! I shouldn't laugh. I really don't blame her."

"What do mean?"

"Laura advised Blacklock to go long on Tropical Investments a few years ago. She took it in the shorts when we filed for Chapter 11 protection. Almost got fired."

"Oh, I see."

Jack's eyes widened. "There's more."

"What?"

"Laura and I did a torch dance over a long weekend in Las Vegas about the time Blacklock invested."

"So, it's personal?"

Jack shook his head. "Oh yeah, I probably haven't seen the last of her."

In twenty minutes, we exited Interstate 405 at Florence Avenue and headed west towards the rental car return lot at the Los Angeles International Airport. It was mid-afternoon, not a busy time at the airport, so we quickly returned the car and breezed through security in Terminal 4 as we headed to Gate 46C to catch a National Airlines flight back to Dallas. Shortly, our flight started to board and we settled into our seats in the tenth row. I looked out of the window after we took off as we flew over the sand dunes towards the Pacific Ocean and wondered about the future of Jack's start-up and what it would mean to me. Maybe I was getting ahead of myself, but Jack's transcendent financial talents could be a difference maker for me. Maybe that house on the lake west of Austin might be in reach now?

In a few minutes, I put the newspaper down that I was trying to read. My eyes felt heavy and I was exhausted. Then I glanced over at Jack—his eyes were closed and he appeared to be sleeping. Soon, he started to snore. When we reached cruising altitude the flight attendants rolled their carts into aisle and started the dinner service. "What would you like—the chicken or the beef?" asked a tall woman with blond hair.

I raised my hand and shook my head. "No thanks. Just wake me up before we land in Dallas."

She winked at me and continued to roll her cart down the aisle.

CHAPTER 22

The trip to Simi Valley for Demo Day had been a beatdown and I was glad to be home. After Joe and I finished cleaning the dinner dishes, I sat down at the dining room table to review two financial presentations scheduled to be delivered at National Airlines later in the week. Then my cell phone rang. Buddy Johnson, the omnipresent recruiting coordinator and assistant baseball coach for Our Savior's University, was calling. Joe had mentioned over the last month that Buddy's calls had become less frequent and he wondered if that reflected a diminished level of interest. I picked up my phone. "Hello, Buddy."

"Mr. Jones, the coaching staff has reviewed our list of recruits and scholarship availability."

His message and tone sounded a bit ominous so I wasn't sure what to expect next. "Yes, Buddy."

"Recently, a coveted pitcher from outside of Chicago called the head coach and expressed a profound interest in playing for Our Savior's. All of the coaches scouted him at the showcase in Jupiter, Florida two weeks ago."

"Ok?"

I could hear Buddy take a deep breath before he spoke. "The head coach feels he is a difference maker who would be in the starting rotation as soon as he steps on campus."

"So, how does that impact us?"

"What I am trying to say is that he demands a full scholarship. We can't give him a partial like everyone else."

"Does this impact Joe?"

There was a brief pause before Buddy continued. "Well, I am sorry to say, it does. If we give the pitcher a full ride then we don't have any money left for Joe."

"But, you said—"

"What I said is that we like Joe and would try hard to make it work."

I shook my head and didn't know what to say next. There was a noise from the kitchen and I looked up as Joe walked in. His face was expressionless. Maybe he heard parts of the conversation. I put my hand over the speaker on my phone and whispered to Joe, "Buddy is on the phone. Looks like Our Savior's doesn't have a scholarship for you."

Joe's head dropped. The color left his face and he turned to me. "But he told me…"

Then Buddy said, "Mr. Jones, are you still there?"

I removed my hand from over the speaker. "Yes I am, but I don't think we have anything more to talk about."

"Mr. Jones, I would appreciate a couple of more minutes of your time. Well...I may have a solution. What if Joe comes to Our Savior's as a preferred walk-on? He would be on the team from day one. No tryout would be necessary. His locker would be with all of the scholarship players."

"What?"

"Nobody besides me would know he was a walk-on."

I laughed to myself after hearing Buddy's proposal. Our Savior's was a very expensive private school in West Central Texas. Tuition, books, room and board would run over sixty-five thousand dollars a year. I couldn't afford to send him there without obtaining scholarship assistance.

"Buddy, the only people who would know Joe was a walk-on would be you, me and my banker! I sure wish you could have told us this earlier in the recruiting process. Thank you for your time. Good day."

"Nice speaking to you, Mr. Jones."

Joe and I remained silent for a couple of minutes. I put my cell phone down on the table. "Well, I guess we're going to have to jump-start the recruiting process. It's late and most of the teams have allocated all of their available scholarship dollars. I'll call Mike Rizzo to get some ideas."

At that moment, all I wanted to do was kick Buddy Johnson's fat ass. I had been warned about duplicitous coaches and Buddy in particular, but I never thought Joe would be the one to end up on the short end. I needed to collect my thoughts and regroup. Maybe my two-day trip to Mexico with Jack would help to clear my head.

CHAPTER 23

"Bienvenidos a Morelia!" the flight attendant announced as we taxied to the terminal.

Jack looked out the window and then glanced over at me across the aisle, "It's great to be back in Mexico!"

In minutes, we picked up our bags and headed to the center of the terminal. "Where are we going to meet Jorge?" I asked.

"Outside of the Café Punta del Cielo," Jack responded.

We walked another thirty feet and saw Jorge Tatis, Jr. He looked just as Jack described him—he stood 6'2", skinny, long black hair, a drooping mustache and multiple gold rings on his fingers. Jack walked up to him and extended his hand. "Hola mi amigo, como estas?"

Jorge smiled. "Señor Jack, nice to see you. My car is parked in front. It's a short drive."

Jack looked over at me. "Jorge, I would like you

to meet my business associate Lonny Jones."

"Señor Lonny, it is a pleasure. Any amigo of Jack's is a friend of mine."

We shook hands and Jorge slapped me on the back. Then he motioned to the left and we proceeded to the front exit and on to the parking lot. Jorge's green Land Rover sat directly in front of us. Jack got in the front passenger seat next to Jorge and I settled in the back seat directly behind him. We headed west towards Morelia on Highway 120.

"We will be in Morelia in thirty minutes. Señor Lonny, please grab some cold beers for us in the cooler behind you."

The ice-cold beer was delicious. Soon each of us was two beers in. Jack stared out the window as if he were studying the scenery. Then he adjusted himself in his seat before he looked over at Jorge. "So when do I meet Ramirez?"

"Ah, Ramirez 'El Gato Negro'."

"How did he get that moniker?" inquired Jack.

Jorge laughed. "He moves silently, mostly at night."

The smile left Jack's face. "Tell me about this Ramirez guy."

"He's a local player. Moved here from Mexico City five years ago."

"What business is he involved with beside avocados?

A wide grin appeared on Jorge's face. "Everything."

"What?"

Jorge laughed. "Yes, mi amigo, everything."

"Where am I going to meet him?"

"At a cantina in Morelia at nine tonight."

"What advice do you have for me?"

"Señor Jack, a couple of things—do all of your talking in the cantina and don't bring your money—that needs to come later."

Jack nodded knowingly. "Can Ramirez be trusted?"

"Well...only if he respects you."

Morelia was a beautiful city with architecture from the 1500s. Many of the older buildings looked like they had been built with red stone. Our hotel sat across the street from a cathedral. Jorge parked in front of the hotel's main entrance. Then Jack and I grabbed our bags from the back of the Land Rover. "I will be back at eight-forty-five and we will walk to the cantina. It's a couple of blocks to the south." Jorge waved and departed.

The old hotel had a large lobby but only one elevator. We checked in and headed up to our rooms. Jack settled into room 502 while I relaxed directly across the hall in 503. The room was clean but all of the furniture looked fifty years old. I was tired from the journey and decided to take a short nap. The springs in the bed squeaked loudly when I rolled over.

At eight forty-five I heard someone knocking on Jack's door. "Señor Jack, it's time to meet Ramirez."

I opened my door and quickly joined Jorge and Jack in the hall. Jorge reached into the pocket in his jacket and then handed each of us a Smith & Wesson snub-nosed revolver. "Do you really think this is necessary," I asked.

"Keep it in your pocket just in case," responded Jack.

The elevator arrived in a couple of minutes and we were on our way to the cantina to meet Ramirez. The two-block walk took five minutes and we entered the cantina. A very charming lady with long black hair wearing a colorful dress smiled at us. She briefly studied our faces. "Hello, you're a long way from the United States. Is all of your party here?"

"Si, si, we are here to meet Mr. Ramirez," said Jorge.

"Ah yes, he is expecting you. Please follow me."

We followed the lady into the main dining room and walked towards a corner table. Ramirez sat alone. He stood around 5'10" and probably weighed two hundred and fifty pounds. His jet-black hair fell almost to his shoulders. Two men stood ten feet behind the table. Both had bulges underneath their sport coats.

Ramirez looked up from his plate of enchiladas as we approached. Then he rose and extended his hand towards Jack. Jack smiled and they shook hands. "Señor Ramirez, mi nombre es Jack Heygood."

Ramirez nodded and his eyes twinkled. "Jack Heygood, nice to meet you," said Ramirez with a heavy East Coast accent.

He didn't acknowledge Jorge or me and continued to focus completely on Jack. Maybe this was only going to be a boss-to-boss conversation? Jack stood directly in front of Ramirez. "You must have spent some time on the East Coast. New York?"

"Yes, I was born in New Jersey and moved to Mexico City when I was thirteen."

"Why did you leave New Jersey?"

I glanced at Jorge, the smile disappeared from his face and his eyes widened. Ramirez's face reddened and his eyes narrowed. He looked like he could explode. Then he slammed his fist on the table. The dishes rattled and beer spilled on the table. The other customers in the cantina stared. A few quickly stood up and hastily walked towards the exit. Ramirez glared at Jack and screamed, "Because your government deported my family for no reason!"

The two men standing behind Ramirez reached into their sport coats but didn't reveal their guns. I gripped the snub-nosed revolver in my pants pocket. Jack and Ramirez stood toe-to-toe and neither one blinked. After thirty seconds of awkward silence, a grin appeared on Ramirez's face and he started to laugh. Maybe Jack had passed the test?

Ramirez gestured at the table. "Please, amigos have a seat."

Jack, Jorge and I joined Ramirez at the table. We started off with a couple of rounds of tequila shots. All of the time, Ramirez remained completely focused on Jack—almost as if Jorge and I were not even present. After exchanging some small talk about local fishing opportunities, Ramirez leaned forward. "Jack, tell me how your operation will work."

"I have an option to buy all of the avocado production on three-hundred and fifty acres. The temperature is perfect and avocados can be grown year-around. All of the fruit will be packaged, pre-cooled and refrigerated at Jorge's distribution center prior to shipment. I have leased a fleet of five refrigerated semi-trailer trucks to transport the fruit to my Dallas distribution center. One grocery store chain in North Texas has agreed to buy all of my fruit at very attractive prices."

"Very good, I am sure Jorge negotiated some very favorable purchase agreements with the farmers," said Ramirez with a laugh.

Jorge chimed in, "Yes, very favorable."

"Jorge and I are partners in everything so we're partners. Do you have any problem with that, my friend Jack?"

Jack didn't appear surprised by this comment as his facial expression didn't change. I wondered if Jorge had discussed this with him previously.

Jack studied Ramirez's face. "How do you propose to be involved?"

"My men will provide security for your operation and in exchange I will take ten percent of your profits."

"That's very reasonable," responded Jack.

"In addition, we will share your logistics capability. From time-to-time I ship other commodities to the United States."

Jack and I exchanged nervous glances.

"Sounds fair," said Jack.

"Of course, this will not start right way, I want to give your operation time to become established and flourish."

Jacked nodded. "Thank you."

Soon Ramirez finished his enchiladas and wiped his mouth with the cloth napkin. "Thank you for coming to dinner."

This comment seemed kind of funny as only Ramirez had eaten. But the meeting ended and it was time for us to leave. Jack smiled and gave Ramirez a nod before we stood. Jorge remained seated to the left of Ramirez. Then we turned and walked out of the cantina.

"Jack, do you know what you're getting into?" I said as we walked down the sidewalk towards our hotel.

Jack shrugged. "That's pretty much what I expected."

CHAPTER 24

Our nonstop, red-eye National Airlines flight from Morelia landed on-time, just before six in the morning, at DFW Airport. It was Saturday, and the shuttle busses between the terminal and the distant, reduced-rate parking lot were not running frequently. Finally, Jack and I arrived at the parking lot and threw our bags in the trunk of the *Bullitt*. The sun rose in the east as we exited the parking lot and headed towards State Highway 183. Jack looked over at me and said, "I really appreciate your coming with me to Mexico. Could you drop me off at Jerry's warehouse off of Loop 12? I want to see how the preparations are coming."

"Sure, no problem."

I had not been to Jerry's warehouse since last summer when I came to collect money owed me. Jerry was a charming, colorful guy but a horse's ass who could not be trusted. He had been involved in multiple scams last year and had even used his floundering furniture company to launder money for Jack over an extended period. Only one thing was certain—there would be cold beer waiting for us in the warehouse.

We turned south onto Loop 12 and headed to Jerry's warehouse. In minutes we pulled into the loading dock area. The "Elegant Furniture & Fine Art" sign on the side of the warehouse had been painted over and replaced with "JH Fruit Distribution" in large green letters. A large pile of old office furniture and paintings stood abandoned to the side of the warehouse. We walked up the steps and entered through the loading dock doors. All of the old office furniture from the 1970s that previously occupied the warehouse had disappeared.

The warehouse was now air conditioned and partitioned into a number of zones each with industrial-sized, heavy-duty shelves from the floor to the ceiling. We walked another seventy-five feet and were in front of Jerry's office next to his secretary's abandoned cubicle. We looked into the office. There was Jerry—a few inches shorter than six feet and a stocky build with a large head. He wore his blond hair short and had his customary wide grin on his face. He didn't possess a sophisticated appearance with his feet propped up on the desk and a toothpick dangling from the corner of his mouth but rather had the look of someone emerging from the piney woods of East Texas. He was recently divorced and now remarried with a baby boy. Next to Jerry, sat a baby-faced Asian man wearing a baseball hat backwards who looked like he was probably in his early forties.

"Gentlemen, I'd like you to meet my graveyard shift manager, Jong 'Johnny' Kwon. Johnny was a supply sergeant in the Korean Army."

"Nice meet you," said Johnny with a heavy accent as we shook hands.

Jerry grinned at us. "It's five o'clock somewhere, may I get you guys a brew?"

We nodded affirmatively and Jerry quickly grabbed four sixteen-ounce, ice-cold beers from the refrigerator behind his desk. Jack and I sat down next to Johnny across the desk from Jerry. The beer was delicious. Jack gazed out the door of the office and then looked at Jerry. "How are the preparations coming?"

"The five air-conditioning units were installed a couple of days ago. We plan to keep two zones at 5 to 8° C and another at 10 to 25° C to control softening."

"Outstanding! Have you started to hire the warehouse workers?"

"Yes, interviews are in progress. I will have three shifts. The first two have ten people while the graveyard shift has five."

"Jerry, you have done a fine job. I knew I could count on you."

Jerry took a quick look at me and then gazed back at Jack. "Thanks, what about Lonny? Is he on the team?"

"Not yet. He says he's in an unofficial, consultative role at the moment—whatever the hell that means?" said Jack as he chuckled and rolled his eyes.

I retorted, "I'm just an airline guy that doesn't want to get shot!"

Jack and Jerry started to laugh. Then Jerry got up and grabbed four more beers. After he popped the top of his beer, Jerry looked over at Jack and me. "Well, what about baseball?"

"Mark and Joe are returning to the Dallas Generals this summer," said Jack.

Jerry shook his head. "You know, I called Coach Espinosa a month ago. I tried to smoke a peace pipe with him and asked if he would give Skylar a second chance. After all, he didn't do anything wrong. It was all my fault. I was the one who embezzled from the team's funds."

Jerry's chutzpah amused me. "What did Coach Espinosa say?"

"He started screaming and swearing. He wanted to fight me. The guy has no sense of humor. I'm not sure he would be a good influence on Skylar anyway."

"That's too bad. People need to let go of what happened in the past," remarked Jack.

I shook my head in amusement. Both Jack and Jerry could lay it on pretty thick.

"So what are you guys going to do this summer?" I asked.

"I'm going to coach a bunch of kids from Skylar's school. We won't be elite but we should be competitive. On a good day, we might even be able to give the Generals a game."

Jerry took a gulp of beer. "Are your boys going to play college ball?"

Jack looked down and then glanced over at me. My head hurt and I struggled to get the words out, "Our Savior's was a possibility until recently when they pulled their verbal offer. A few recruiting coordinators have called so I think there's interest, but we haven't seen any paper on the table."

There was a brief awkward pause. Then Jack looked over at Jerry. "I've appointed myself Mark's lead negotiator."

We all laughed. Somehow that move didn't surprise anybody.

Jack waved his hands and grinned. "I've got twenty coaches on speed dial and I call them every week whether they like it or not."

Jerry nodded and asked, "Well?"

"I'm starting to feel some love, but Mark better have a helluva senior year."

Jack finished the last of his second beer and looked around at everyone. "The beer was great but I could use some breakfast."

Johnny nodded enthusiastically and Jerry quickly responded, "I'm in."

We walked outside and sat down in Johnny's F150. "So, where do you want to go?" I inquired.

Johnny looked over at me. "Eat free."

"Huh?" responded Jack.

Jerry laughed for a few seconds. "Breakfast is Johnny's favorite meal and we eat free every morning."

Jack shook his head. "How do you do that?"

A big smile appeared on Jerry's face. "We crash the complimentary breakfast buffets at the local hotels and motels."

"That certainly shows a sense of style, Jerry. Have you guys ever been caught?" I asked.

"We've had a few close scrapes but then Johnny puts that baby smile on his face and goes into his 'I'm a Korean tourist and don't understand you' spiel and everyone feels sorry for him. A couple of times, they even cooked him breakfast after the free buffet closed."

We all burst out laughing. Jack glanced over at Johnny and then turned to Jerry. "Where did you meet this guy?"

Jerry laughed for a few seconds and raised his eyebrows. "Well, I was waiting to get the 'all-inclusive' special at a Korean massage parlor over on Harry Hines Boulevard near Walnut Hill Lane and started talking to him in the waiting area. He appeared to be just another customer waiting for a massage but he managed the operation. He's actually one of the owners."

"Really?" Jack remarked as he glanced over at Johnny.

"Yeah, he won a ten-percent stake in the massage parlor during a poker game."

In a few minutes Johnny slowed his truck down as we turned left into the Best Southern Inn Express parking lot.

CHAPTER 25

Skip drove his dull-red Alfa Romeo into the driveway on the side of his bungalow after a long day at work. It was almost nine and the sun had set. The yard was completely dark and no lights were on inside. He pulled his keys out of the ignition and grabbed the fifth of Fred Beamer Kentucky Straight Bourbon Whiskey on the seat next to him. Then he unscrewed the top, took a belt and then closed his eyes for a few seconds. After sitting for a few minutes, he grabbed the bottle and walked to the side door of his house that opened towards the driveway. He turned the unlocked knob. Skip took two steps inside and saw a figure seated at his kitchen table.

"Skip, don't turn on the lights. Come over here and sit down."

Skip jumped. "What do you want?"

He took a couple of steps toward the table but tripped on the kitchen rug and just caught himself before he hit the floor.

After sitting down, Skip looked at the Black Widow and there was a long pause. "I've given you everything you wanted. Please don't hurt me."

"You've been a good boy so far but you know I could ruin your career at National Airlines and make you the laughing stock of Dallas anytime I want."

"Yeah, I know."

"What's National's next move in the negotiations with Global?"

Skip held up his hands just above the table. "Nothing has changed in the last two weeks."

"Sure it has... You're turning into a big disappointment," replied the Black Widow.

The Black Widow stood up and walked around the kitchen table. Skip turned in his chair and put up his hands in some sort of defensive posture. "Please don't hurt me."

"If nothing has changed, why does Global continue to push back our meeting with them?"

The Black Widow smiled at Skip and turned sideways—almost as if to get into position to deliver a karate kick. Skip quickly grabbed the bottle of Fred Beamer Kentucky Straight Bourbon Whiskey in his right hand, jumped up and let fly at the Black Widow's head. The bottle shattered on impact just as the Black Widow started to spin. She took two steps forward and then collapsed on the kitchen floor. Blood gushed from her head onto the rug.

"You wimp!" she screamed. "I'll kill you."

Skip ran out the side door into the driveway, jumped into his Alfa Romeo and quickly backed up onto the street. His tires screeched as he weaved down the road at a high speed narrowly missing his neighbors walking their dog.

CHAPTER 26

Meetings filled my calendar at National Airlines from seven-thirty in the morning to five in the afternoon. My nine o'clock meeting with Skip on Project Green Field was scheduled in his office. I walked up the stairs to the fifth floor and over to Skip's corner office in the North Wing. As I approached, I could see through the window that ran the length of his office. The lights were off and the office was dark and unoccupied. I walked down to his administrative assistant's cubicle. "Good morning Judy. I have a nine o'clock with Skip. Any idea when he will be in?"

"He hasn't called in. Maybe he had an offsite meeting or a doctor's appointment."

"It's not like him to miss meetings."

"Yeah, that's true. I'll call you when he gets in."

"Thanks."

I returned to my office to read the hundred new emails that had arrived and prep for my next meeting. The rest of my schedule had gone to plan and I returned to my office for a staff meeting with my managers at the end of the day. Before the staff meeting started, I closed my office door and called Judy. "Any news from Skip?"

"He just texted and said he was very sick. He may be out tomorrow too."

"Thanks, maybe I should give him a call?"

"No, don't do that. Skip said he didn't want to be disturbed."

"That's fair. I'll talk to him on the flip side."

Sixty minutes later I walked out the door and headed home. My ancient Schwinn Collegiate five-speed bike had been repaired at Spoke City Bike Shop in Highland Park and was ready to be picked up. I decided to swing by the shop on way home. I got on Lovers Lane and headed east. Skip's bungalow was located on the next side street. For some reason I turned onto Skip's block. I stopped in front of the bungalow located on the west side of the street. There was no sign of Skip. Maybe he needed some medicine or groceries? In thirty seconds I stepped onto the porch. I knocked twice and there was no answer. The door must not have been completely shut because my knocks pushed it open a couple of inches. I waited several minutes for Skip to respond but heard nothing. My cell phone rang and I looked down to my pocket to grab it and answer the call. Then I noticed the trail of blood drops from the door down to the steps on the porch. Someone left Skip's house and was bleeding. I pushed the door open. The trail of blood ran back towards the kitchen. I took several steps forward and looked into the kitchen. You could smell the whiskey. A broken bottle of Fred Beamer Bourbon Whiskey laid on the floor with glass strewn all over. A bloody handprint was visible on the floor in front of the table. The rug was soaked in blood. This was a mess for the police to sort out.

I picked up my phone to call Vince Truex. It rang twice. "Vince Truex here."

"This is Lonny. I am here at Skip Wise's bungalow. There has been an accident or a crime. Blood is all over."

"Okay, don't touch anything. I will be there in ten minutes."

I sat on the front porch and waited for Vince to arrive. After five minutes, Vince pulled his car into the driveway. He quickly walked over. "Show me what you told me about on the phone."

"Sure, follow me."

We retraced my steps to the kitchen. Vince surveyed the scene. "Looks like somebody got hit with a bottle. The blood is mostly dry. This must have taken place several hours ago, maybe even yesterday. Have you talked to Skip today?"

"He didn't come to work today. His text to his admin said he was too sick to come into the office."

"Anything else?"

"Yeah, he didn't want to be disturbed today."

"This could be a crime scene. I need to get the lab boys down here."

"I hope Skip isn't hurt."

"Anything is possible. Go home. I'll call you when I know more."

• • •

A couple of hours later, I washed the last dirty dinner plate and sat down to watch some major

119

league baseball on the sports channel. Then my phone rang. Vince's phone number displayed on the caller ID. "Hello, have you turned up anything?" I asked.

"Yes, the lab team just finished their preliminary investigation."

"What did they find?"

"We likely had a female and a male in the house when the incident occurred."

"How did they determine that?"

"Standard forensic techniques were used to establish sex."

"How did that work?"

"Females have higher amino acid levels and higher ridge density in their finger prints."

"Interesting, you cops are pretty smart."

"Yeah, I know...The male's finger prints were all over the house so I am guessing they were Skip's."

"What about the female?"

"The female's finger prints were found on the side door knob, kitchen table and kitchen floor. The bloody hand print on the floor belonged to the female."

"Wow."

"The neck of the whiskey bottle was found intact. Only the male's finger prints were detected on it. We found one of piece of glass with the female's finger prints—a small, bloody shard with membrane and a ten-inch strand of black hair attached was in a small pool of blood in the living room near the front door."

"What do you think happened?"

"Based on these preliminary findings, the male hit the female in the head with the whiskey bottle, knocking her to the kitchen floor. She eventually stood up, walked towards the front door and removed the embedded glass in her head before exiting."

"Vince, I'll take your analysis a step further based upon what Skip told us previously. I bet Skip and the Black Widow tangled and Skip won his first round of the fight."

"That's certainly a possibility."

"All of this helps to explain Skip's absence from work. He may be laying low until this cools down."

"If you see Skip, tell him to call the Dallas Police as soon as possible. We need to sort this out."

I shook my head. "With the Black Widow and the two guys who shot at us in the Screwball parking lot around the edges of this thing, nobody is safe."

CHAPTER 27

Dad's prostate procedure was only supposed to take ninety minutes but he had been gone for two hours. What could have happened? Was he alright? I sat down in the visitor's chair in his room and tried to read the newspaper. Then a nurse walked in and surveyed the medical equipment. "When will he be done with the procedure?" I asked.

"Your father is in the recovery room now. The doctor will be here to talk to you in a few minutes," said the nurse matter-of-factly.

I looked at my watch. Twenty minutes had passed. The door suddenly swung open and the doctor strode into Pete's room still wearing his light blue scrubs followed closely by two medical students holding notepads. "Mr. Jones, your father is doing very well and should be back here in half an hour."

"How did the procedure go?"

"The focal laser ablation was successful. I spent more time than expected destroying the cancer near the bladder wall."

"Will he be able to go home today?"

"No, we'll hold him for observation overnight."

The doctor nodded and left the room with the two medical students. Soon two nurses wheeled Dad into the room on a gurney. His eyes were shut and he seemed to be asleep. The nurse at the head of the gurney said, "Mr. Jones, you're back in your room. We're going to move you back onto the bed now."

The two nurses grunted as they slid him onto the bed. Dad looked up at me for several seconds without saying a word. Then his eyes blinked several times. "Son, am I ok?"

"Sure, Dad. The doctor said he destroyed all of the cancer."

"That's good. Can we go home now?"

"No, not until the morning."

Dad frowned, looked down at the tube from the catheter and shook his head. "I hate staying in hospitals."

I patted Dad on the arm to console him. "You may have some visitors today."

Dad smiled briefly. "That's great. Who's coming?"

"A couple of guys from the fire station."

"Anyone else?"

"Joe will be here later. Jack said he planned to see you."

"Jack?"

"Jack Heygood."

Dad grimaced. "I told you not to have anything to do with him. He's nothing but trouble."

"Jack likes you and wants to see how you're doing."

His face reddened and he started breathing

hard. "He almost got you killed last year. They're shooting at him this year. Will you ever listen to your dad?"

"Dad, it'll be ok."

He frowned and pulled the sheet over his face. Ten minutes later we heard two loud knocks on the door. Dad pulled down the sheet covering his face just as Jack walked into the room with a disarming ear-to-ear smile on his face. "Well, well, how's Pete doing?"

"I'm fine...thank you very much," said Dad as a slight smile appeared on his face.

Then Dad continued, "Jack, I have been thinking about you. The Monsignor over at Cardinal Mahony wants to see you. He thinks he can help to get your life back on track."

Jack raised his eyebrows. "I'm not sure if I'm interested. I don't need a sermon."

"But the Monsignor presided at Wendy's funeral and he got to know Mark."

Jack shrugged and paused for a moment. "Look Pete, I'm a Baptist. Wendy was the Catholic in the family."

"The Monsignor knows that. He just wants to help."

"I really don't think I need help—"

I interjected, "He helped me get through the hard times after Joan walked out."

Jack shook his head and said nothing for a minute. Then he glanced at us. "Well, I appreciate your concern. I think I'll be leaving now. All the best, Pete," said Jack as he waved and walked out the door.

Pete's mouth flattened and he shook his head. "I don't know what to think about that Jack Heygood."

"Dad, you did everything you could."

"Yeah, I know. I just wish he would listen to me."

I held up my hands. "Jack marches to his own drummer."

CHAPTER 28

The conference call with Jack's investors was scheduled to begin at seven tonight. Jack planned to do the call out of Jerry's spacious office at the warehouse equipped with a speaker phone and conference table. Seed investors Vic Moskowicz from Blue Ridge Partners and Pete Stubbs of Pine Tree Capital each invested five-hundred thousand dollars and would be on the call along with a couple of other people who were not identified. Jim Taggart and I were invited and decided to participate on a lark. We were curious if Jack had just produced a lot of smoke or actually accomplished something. The warehouse was a little bit out of my way home from National Airlines but the call would likely be much more amusing than anything you could find on TV. Jack had distributed his presentation earlier by email.

Taggart and I sat opposite from Jack and Jerry at the conference table. Jack looked around the room at each of us. "I really want the investors to feel it."

Jerry had bewildered expression on his face. "What?"

Jack stood up. "Let's project it and I will stand as if everyone is in the room. My passion will not come through if I'm sitting and reading."

Jack was on a roll. His demeanor reminded me of the early years at Tropical Investments when his salesmanship was unmatched.

Jerry quickly hooked up a projector to his computer and the first slide of the deck displayed on the wall. Jack stood on the left side of the screen. "Jerry, let's get this call going."

We were the first on the bridge and then quickly joined by Vic and Pete.

"Shall we begin?" boomed Jack.

"Slide one. I'm happy to announce that our proof of concept is a total success. Let's review our accomplishments over the last ninety days. First, we were able to obtain the necessary approvals on both sides of the border to commence this operation. Usually, those processes are very slow and involve a lot of red tape. However, we achieved them at breakneck speed."

Jim Taggart and I exchanged glances and laughed. I wondered if there was a more subtle meaning in Jack's statement.

Jack gestured with his hands as if he were playing to an audience. "Slide two. Second, we stood up the company. Thirty tons of avocados from our fields in Mexico were successfully shipped to our customers in North Texas. We transported the product to our distribution center in Michoacán and then on to our facility off of Loop 12 here in Dallas. Finally, we delivered the product to our customer here in Dallas. Our logistics capabilities were validated."

Jack paused for a moment to catch his breath and Vic Moskowicz interjected, "That's outstanding work! Your team's performance is top-notch. You've surpassed my wildest expectations."

Pete Stubbs added, "I completely agree with Vic. Great job."

Jack grinned from ear-to-ear as if he knew the investors were eating out of the palm of his hand. He took a deep breath. "Slide three. I don't want you to have to just take my word that the customer was satisfied. So, I have asked Chet Brooks, VP of Operations for the BEB Grocery Chain to join us and provide his thoughts on the product and the service provided. Chet, please go ahead."

"Thanks Jack. Previously, we were never able to get as much product as we wanted when we wanted it. Also, the product received was not always of the highest quality so much was lost due to spoilage. That's why I entered into this preliminary agreement. Jack has delivered quality product on schedule at economical prices. This preliminary relationship has been a great success for BEB. I believe that all of this was achieved through Jack's decisive and visionary—if I might say ballsy— leadership."

Jack closed his eyes and nodded in agreement. "Thanks Chet."

This conference call was certainly more amusing than anything I could have watched on TV. Taggart had a grin on his face and whispered to me, "When do we get the popcorn?"

Chet continued, "It has worked out so well that I want to expand our relationship and have Jack supply all of our stores in North Texas. If that goes well, then on to all of the Southwest and then the nation."

Jack puffed up his cheeks. "Thank you, Chet. Slide four. We designed our business model to scale up to service virtually any level of potential customer demand."

Pete stubbed jumped in. "This is extremely encouraging news. The question is not if we should expand but rather how quickly we expand."

We were watching a command performance by Jack. "Slide five. In the coming weeks I plan to get back to Vic and Pete to discuss our plans to obtain Series A funding."

Jack had a triumphant look on his face as he waved his hands. "Are there any more questions?"

Vic responded, "No. Thanks for the very informative update. Good work Jack."

The call ended. Jerry had an ear-to-ear smile and jumped up. "I'm feelin' it!"

Jack screamed, "Yes! Yes! Yes!" and then walked around the room and gave everyone a high-five.

Jerry smiled and looked around the table. "Would anyone like a beer?"

Everyone quickly raised their hands and soon a chorus of beer bottles being popped could be heard. Johnny Kwon had been sitting in the corner and had remained quiet throughout the call. Jack gazed at him for a moment. "Well Johnny, what do you think?"

Johnny had that baby-face smile and looked at Jack. "Wow, this is bigger than I thought. Someday it might end up being more lucrative than my massage parlor on Harry Hines Boulevard!"

Jack broke up laughing and then raised his beer to make a toast. "To Johnny!"

Everyone else laughed and briefly held their beers high. Then we clinked each other's beers, repeated Jack's toast and took a drink.

CHAPTER 29

William Clayton's retrial was set to begin in a couple of months. The Justice Department's legal team scheduled a series of meetings with Jack to review his prior testimony at Clayton's initial trial and discuss anticipated questions from Clayton's legal team that would now be led by the celebrated defense lawyer D. Clarence Shapiro. Shapiro had a flamboyant court-room demeanor and gained notoriety for his destructive treatment of opposing witnesses during cross examination. Al Stephens and the Federal Prosecutor handling William Clayton's retrial told Jack that exhaustive pre-trial preparation would be needed in order to withstand the anticipated onslaught from Shapiro. Jack had asked Jim Taggart and me to attend the initial meeting to be held at the Earl Campbell Federal Building on Commerce Street in downtown Dallas.

We arrived fifteen minutes prior to the meeting and were ushered into the same fourth floor conference room where Taggart had negotiated Jack's pardon months ago. All three of us sat with our backs to the window on the south side of the room. Jim glanced over at Jack. "You know, I'm not here in any official capacity just as a favor to Lonny."

"I guess one hundred thousand dollars doesn't buy much these days," retorted Jack.

"That fee covered only the cost of getting you out of prison. Nothing more."

The door opened. Al Stephens and the Federal Prosecutor in charge of the retrial entered and sat across the conference room table from us. Stephens looked over at us. "As you know, Shapiro is going to be a very difficult adversary. He is rude, ruthless and a bully. Almost like a python that squeezes you tighter every time you open your mouth to breath. If we are to prevail, we must be totally prepared for his tactics."

The Federal Prosecutor looked directly at Jack. "Your earlier testimony was very compelling and integral to securing the convictions but Shapiro has had months to review it and devise defensive strategies. He will probe all of the potential weaknesses in your testimony and attack you personally."

Jack looked around the room and the sides of his mouth curled up. "Now that I have my pardon and launched a very successful international business, I'm not sure if it's in my best interest to testify. I have my reputation to protect and any involvement in Clayton's retrial would only hurt it. Investors need to have confidence in me."

Jim Taggart's jaw dropped and he glared at Jack. "Your testimony was part of the deal to obtain your pardon. I negotiated in good faith. I will completely withdraw from these proceedings if you renege on the deal."

Jack repositioned himself in his chair and took a deep breath. "Jim, you helped to get me out of prison but I think I've got it from this point. Testifying at the retrial would only sully my reputation with the venture capital community."

Al Stephens had taken this conversation in but said nothing to this point. "Mr. Taggart, I appreciate your honesty. You are a man of integrity."

Then Stephens glared at Jack. "Heygood, I always thought you were capable of doing something this stupid."

Jack leaned back in his chair and laughed.

Stephens growled at Jack, "Did you think I would negotiate away all of my levers?"

The smile left Jack's face and his eyes widened.

"You were found with hundreds of thousands of dollars in cash last year in Florida. My friends at the Internal Revenue Service are very interested and want to investigate. I have done my best to keep them at bay so far but if this deal falls through who knows what could happen? My influence with them could wane and you would be on your own. If you end up serving a federal sentence, then I will make sure it is at a maximum-security facility—Florence, Colorado and Marion, Illinois come to mind—not a white-collar country club."

Jack's eyes moved rapidly back and forth. He looked like a cornered animal. "Ok, ok, I will testify."

Stephens smiled and seemed to enjoy the moment. "Good, tomorrow we'll start reviewing the facts in this case and your prior testimony at Clayton's first trial."

The Federal Prosecutor nodded his head. "William Clayton is out of jail on a million-dollar bond and living on his yacht moored in Palm Beach. He may not want to return to prison—"

Jack interrupted, "I know Clayton well. He's capable of anything. What you guys have turned up on him so far related to Tropical Investments is only the tip of the iceberg. His criminal involvement extends way beyond Tropical." Jack gulped and continued, "Yeah, he may not want me to testify."

Stephens laughed. "There is a long list of people that may want to kill you—Tropical investors, William Clayton, maybe even your Mexican business partners and probably others."

"I want protection...at least until the trial," stammered Jack.

"That seems fair. We don't want anything to happen to you so I will make sure US Marshals guard you around the clock. Of course, that precludes any trips to Mexico."

CHAPTER 30

The Generals' kickoff lunch was scheduled to begin at twelve-thirty at a barbeque restaurant off of LBJ Freeway near the former site of Valley View Mall. General Manager Mike Rizzo and Coaches Ronnie and Stan White would discuss the schedule, player fees and goals for the upcoming select baseball season. All of the players including those from out of town planned to attend. Joe and I backed out of the driveway at twelve fifteen for the short drive. Just as we passed Maggie's former house down the street my cell phone started to ring. I looked at the caller ID—it was Buddy Johnson. We had not talked for several months since he withdrew Joe's athletic scholarship offer from Our Savior's. I debated if I should pick up the call. Why not? What was there to lose?

I looked over towards Joe and answered. "Hello, Buddy. This is a surprise."

"Mr. Jones, thank you very much for taking my

call."

Joe shook his head from side to side and had a disgusted look on his face.

I paused for a moment. "Yes, what can I do for you?"

"I am very sorry for how things turned out when we last talked. Joe is a good kid."

I made a left turn off of Royal Lane onto Preston Road and headed north before I resumed the conversation. "Why did you call?"

"Well, there have been some developments that I wanted to discuss with you."

"Such as?"

"You remember the pitcher from Chicago that committed to play for us?"

"Yes, the one whose full scholarship offer left you with no money to offer Joe?"

"He injured his arm throwing in an Illinois State High School playoff game."

"So?" I inquired.

Buddy paused for a few seconds. "He will have to sit out next season after he has surgery."

"So he will redshirt at Our Savior's next season?"

"Not exactly, we recommended that he attend a local junior college a few miles away from Our Savior's. He could still come over to campus any time he wants and would feel like he's a part of the team...but would not be supported by one of our athletic scholarships. The following year, he can transfer over and play on the team."

"Let me get this straight. You pulled his scholarship offer because of the injury and now have money available to give to someone who can help you win games next spring?"

"Yes, that's sort of the bottom line."

"What is the pitcher going to do?"

"Well, unfortunately he did not completely grasp the benefits of attending the local junior college while still getting to experience college life at Our Savior's. We're not exactly sure what his plans are."

"So, how does that impact Joe?"

"Given the current availability of funding, we are prepared to offer Joe a scholarship that will cover twenty-five percent of his expenses at Our Savior's. It would be guaranteed for one year. We meet with the players after each season to discuss their performance and scholarship allocations for the next year."

I glanced over at Joe. "Well, this is a surprising development."

"Mr. Jones, I know Joe may be considering some state schools at this point but Our Savior's provides a unique, nourishing environment that enables our student athletes to flourish. We instill the right family values."

"Buddy, could you please send Joe a scholarship contract that spells all of this out? Then he can make a decision."

"Thank you, Mr. Jones. It's in the mail!"

I quickly hung up the phone just as we pulled into the restaurant parking lot. Joe laughed and looked over to me. "I can hardly wait to tell Buddy to go to hell."

As we got out of the car and started walking towards the restaurant, I said, "Well, don't do that just yet. We need to make sure another option materializes that you like."

Joe nodded. "I got it. Some of the college coaches have told me that a few of their top recruits may sign contracts with professional teams after the draft and that scholarship money could free up. So, I may need to wait till June to make a final decision about college."

"You are in good shape since you applied to a number of colleges and have already been accepted. You have a plan even if college baseball doesn't pan out."

We walked into the restaurant and saw most of the familiar faces from last year's team that came in second in the National Championship Tournament in Phoenix last summer. Coaches Ronny Espinosa and Stan White came over and extended their hands. Ronny grinned and said, "Joe, we are expecting big things from you this season."

"Thanks Ronny. It's nice to see all of the guys."

A serious expression appeared on Ronny's face and he whispered, "What about Josh Baker? Is he going to play with us?"

Joe sighed. "I don't know. His dad wants him to play college football. Last week, he called and said he wants to sign a professional baseball contract."

Ronny glanced over at Stan and then back at Joe. "I'm hearing he will go in the first round. Given their situation with his dad not having a steady job and being in and out of jail, how could they turn down a million dollars?"

Stan White grimaced. "Yeah, I don't think he ends up playing on the Generals this summer." Then he turned to Joe. "You are going to have to step up this year and help fill the pitching void."

"Coach, I'm ready," responded Joe.

Loud laughter could be heard at an adjacent table where most of Joe's teammates had congregated. Joe turned and walked over.

I took several steps into the restaurant and glanced to my right—Mark Heygood's aunt sat alone at a corner table. She smiled and motioned to me as I walked towards her. "You know Lonny, I'm very sorry about the way we barged into your house. It wasn't fair to you or Jim Taggart but we were desperate."

"Sharon, you did what you had to do." I laughed and continued, "Jim got over it after Jack paid him one-hundred thousand dollars!"

"Please sit down. Is Maggie here? I want to apologize to her too."

I maneuvered into the booth and paused for a moment. "Maggie and I aren't together anymore."

Sharon's eyes widened then she looked down. "I'm so sorry."

"At this point, I think it's for the best."

My head started to hurt. Both of us wanted to change the subject. "So tell me, how is Mark doing?"

"Better, much better. He and Jack are finally starting to communicate but it will take some time for them to get back together. I think it's for the best that Mark finishes high school in Oklahoma City—he's not ready to live with Jack and his girlfriend."

"He's welcome to stay with Joe and me this summer."

Sharon nodded. Then I took a sip of water. "Any idea where Mark will go to school?"

Sharon sighed. "Unless something happens soon, Mark's baseball career will end this summer."

CHAPTER 31

Joe and I just finished cleaning up after dinner and I sat down to sort through all of the junk mail that arrived today. The house was much quieter after Maggie moved out and I started to think about her. I had replayed that unfortunate incident when we ran into Jack and Sunny at the mall over and over many times in my head. Maybe the result could have been different if I would have handled the situation better. I tried to explain to Maggie that nothing really happened between Sunny and me but she didn't want to listen. Perhaps she was correct when she told me that we weren't right for each other. Then my cell phone rang; Vince Truex's phone number displayed on the caller ID.

"Hello, Vince. How are you doing?"

"Fine. I'm not calling you about Jack or Skip."

I was perplexed. "What's up?"

"I heard that you and Maggie broke up."

"Well, actually we broke up a couple of months

ago. We ran into Jack and Sunny at the mall. Sunny brought up last summer and made it sound that I pursued her for sex. She wanted to create problems between Maggie and me."

"Well, you did play a role in getting her and Jack arrested," responded Vince.

"I explained all of that to Maggie but her feelings were hurt and she didn't want to listen."

"Maggie is a good woman. Don't give up."

I couldn't sit down so I got up and started walking around the house. "She moved all of her belongings out of the house. We haven't talked in over a month."

Vince paused for several seconds. "This was all my fault since I prodded you to take a side trip to Delray Beach and snoop around—the sort of investigative work that I can't do. I put you in a bad situation."

I shook my head and sat down at the kitchen table. "That's water under the bridge. It probably doesn't matter now anyway."

"If you don't mind, I'm going to give her a call and try to make this thing right."

"Vince, you're probably wasting your time. I think her mind is made up."

"No problem, I'll let you know how it turns out."

• • •

A couple of weeks later, Vince picked me up and we drove to the parking lot of an upscale Mexican restaurant.

"Vince, I don't think this is a good idea."

"Look, I explained everything to Maggie and she's ready to talk to you."

"I guess it's worth a shot."

We walked into the restaurant. There was no sign of Maggie. After waiting five minutes, the hostess directed us to a booth in the far corner away from the entrance. A waitress walked towards us and leaned over the table. "Would you gentlemen like to order a drink?

"No, not yet. We are waiting for another party."

Fifteen minutes passed and I wondered if Maggie decided not to come. Maybe she had second thoughts after she talked to Vince.

I looked across the table at Vince as he took a sip of water. "Maybe she blew us off?"

"Be patient. The traffic could be bad."

Vince faced the entrance and periodically scanned the waiting area. Then a smile came to his face. "Here she comes."

I turned to see her. As usual, she looked fantastic. Her hair, a little bit longer than I remembered, hung down to her shoulders. Vince sat on the outside of the both seat opposite me so Maggie had no choice but to sit next to me. He looked at both of us. "I'm glad we could get together. I created this mess and hope you guys can put things back together. It was all my fault. You two are good for each other."

I nodded at Vince and glanced over at Maggie. We briefly looked into each other's eyes and Maggie grinned. Then Vince started shuffling in his seat and said, "Would you please excuse me for a minute?"

Vince knew he had done his job and made his way out so we could be alone. I reached over to touch her hand. Soon my hand was gently nestled between both of her hands. We didn't say anything for a few seconds and then I leaned in and gave her a brief kiss on the cheek. She gazed at me. "I'm so sorry for not trusting you. The thought of your being with another woman made me crazy. I just lost it and couldn't think. Will you accept my apology?"

"Yes, I missed you very much over the last few months. I want you back."

I reached over with my free hand and pulled her towards me as I gave her a hug that seemed to last forever.

"Excuse me, sir."

He surprised me. The waiter must have been standing there for a couple of minutes. I quickly glanced at the adjacent tables and all of the customers were staring at us. Maggie blushed.

"Would you like to order now?"

I felt a bit flustered but replied, "I think the lady and I have changed our plans. We will be leaving now."

The waiter seemed annoyed and shook his head. "That will be just fine."

Maggie and I stood up and walked out of the restaurant arm-in-arm as many of the customers glanced over and chuckled. One man seated with his wife and children gave me a thumbs up sign. Soon we were standing in front of her car in the parking lot. Then we passionately kissed for a couple of minutes. Maggie held me tight and looked up. "Can I give you a ride?"

"Yes, I don't want to take the bus."

We sat down in Maggie's car and all I wanted to do was kiss her and feel her arms around me. I gazed into her eyes and leaned in. Then I felt the palms of her hands against my chest, almost as if she was pushing me away.

I didn't know what to think. "Maggie, what's the

matter?"

"Why didn't you tell me the whole story about that woman?"

"I tried, Maggie. Maybe...I missed a few of the details. She doesn't mean anything to me. You are the love of my life."

Maggie looked away. "I found out everything from that woman in the return line at the department store. That was so humiliating."

We locked eyes. "I am so sorry, please forgive me. I'm begging you for a second chance."

Maggie pulled me closer and we embraced. Then she laughed and whispered, "Please take me home tonight."

We drove directly to my house and Maggie pulled up right behind the *Bullitt* in the driveway. Maggie and I walked hand-in-hand to the house and entered through the back door. We embraced and Maggie whispered, "I wonder if Joe is home?"

Before I could say anything we looked up and saw Joe eating a snack at the kitchen table. He had a mischievous grin and laughed. "Yeah, I'm home. It's about time you love birds got back together. It's been kind of rough living here with just Lonny."

Maggie and I laughed and sat down with Joe.

CHAPTER 32

My cell phone started ringing just before eight in the evening. It was Skip. I quickly picked up. "Skip, where are you?"

"We need to talk. We need to talk now," said Skip.

Skip sounded frantic. Should I call Vince Truex immediately? I paused for a moment as I mulled the options. "I can be over at your house in fifteen minutes."

"No, not there."

"Why?"

"I can't go home. They're looking for me."

"Why don't you come over to my house? Joe isn't here."

"No. Veritas knows where you live—they beat up Pete there. Besides, the Black Widow could have figured you out and have your house under surveillance."

"Skip, everything is going to be alright. You

need to calm down."

"For God's sake, how can I be calm?"

"Where are you right now?"

"I'm at a gas station at the corner of Oak Lawn and Maple."

"Don't move. I'll be there in ten minutes."

I got into the *Bullitt* and started driving. Soon I turned south off of Mockingbird onto Maple. In ten minutes I entered the intersection of Maple and Oak Lawn and turned into the gas station. Skip's dull-red Alfa Romeo was parked in front of the gas station away from the pumps. I pulled up along the side. Skip's car was completely packed with suitcases. He stood in the checkout line inside the station so I walked in to talk.

Skip's eyes danced back and forth as he looked at everyone who entered the gas station. "Hi Lonny, thanks for coming. I need to get these energy drinks and a snack."

Skip looked terrible with large black, puffy circles around his eyes. Uncharacteristically, he looked disheveled with his hair uncombed and beard unshaven. I hadn't eaten yet so I thought I might check out the fare in the refrigerated section at the far back of the gas station.

"I'm going to get some food too," I said to Skip as I headed to the back of the store. I examined the contents in the front of the refrigerated food section when Skip joined me after a couple of minutes. After some deliberation, I opened the door and reached in to grab a plastic container with "Fresh Sushi" printed on the top.

Skip looked at me in disbelief. "What are you doing?"

"The sushi looks good."

"Are you crazy? Nobody but nobody eats gas station sushi."

Skip's comments started to annoy me. "I'm sorry this isn't the kind of posh eatery you are used to in Highland Park...the sushi has good color."

Skip winced. "Check the expiration date."

I looked at the fine print on top of the container. "No problem, it's still good for another four hours."

Skip rolled his eyes. "You probably wouldn't mind eating all of your meals at gas stations."

"Ok, so what's your point?"

Skip stood there and said nothing. I could tell he didn't approve. I grabbed a couple packets of soy sauce in case the sushi tasted gamey. After I paid for the sushi, Skip and I stood outside on the sidewalk in front of our cars. Skip's wild look concerned me. "We need to talk. Where should we go?" asked Skip

"Reverchon Park is a couple of blocks south on Maple. Go down to the Turtle Creek intersection and turn west into the park. Joe has played many games on the baseball field at the west end of the park."

Skip followed me as we turned into the park past the recreation center and down the curving road. As we reached the west end we could see the old wooden grandstand built in the 1920s and the elevated north-bound lane of the tollway fifty feet in the air just west of the park. We parked directly to the north of the grandstand and sat down at a shaded picnic table. I pulled out the sushi and started to eat. Skip gave me a couple of disdainful looks before he sat down. I glanced over at him between bites. "Why are you packed?"

Skip surveyed the surrounding area as if he were looking for someone. "I have to leave. I'm in trouble."

"Anything to do with the Black Widow?"

"It's got everything to do with Project Green Field, her and now Veritas."

"What happened?"

"I told you and Vince about her coming on to me at Pedro's."

I wiped some soy sauce off my cheek. "Yes, you guys went home and had kinky sex. Then the next day she came back with pictures. That's where you left it."

Skip paused for a second and had a pained look on his face. "She said the pictures would be sent to my parents and people I work with at National Airlines unless I cooperated."

"What did she want?"

Skip grimaced. "Initially, she just asked me when we were going to meet with Global. Then she asked for much more."

"Why didn't you just tell her to go to hell and take your lumps?"

"At first, the information that I provided had little value and would protect me from being totally embarrassed. But every time I gave her information I just made her hammer bigger. Pretty soon there was no way out. My career would be over. Maybe go to jail."

This story was much worse than I ever could have imagined. "Sorry to hear that."

"I forgot the advice you gave me when I started as an analyst just out of business school."

I leaned back on my seat. "What advice?"

"You told me that if I ever had bad news to report I should 'go ugly early' and communicate the bad news quickly rather than have someone else point it out later."

I nodded in agreement. "Yes, words to live by."

"Well, the last time I saw the Black Widow I broke a bottle of whisky on her head to escape a beating. She's a black belt and told me she enjoyed inflicting pain. You saw me after she kicked my ass before."

"Yeah, your face looked pretty bad."

"Well, after I hit her she said she would kill me."

"So, what do you plan to do now?"

"I have to get out of the middle. I'm resigning from National. My house is on the market." Skip pulled an envelope out of his pocket and handed it to me. "Give this to Bill or Dan."

"Where are you going?"

"I'm driving to California and stay with a fraternity brother from college. He said I could work for his commercial real estate firm. Initially, I'll probably make only twenty percent of what I made at National but it's something and a new start."

We were done eating and got up to leave. I reached out my hand. "Good luck, Skip."

He handed me a key to his house, nodded and jumped into his dull-red Alfa Romeo. Soon he turned his car around in the parking lot to the west of the old wooden grandstand and then headed east out of the park at a high rate of speed. I had hoped to have Skip talk to Vince but that wasn't going to happen now. I called Vince's cell number and he answered after a few rings.

"Hello, Lonny."

"Skip called me and wanted to meet."

"What happened?" inquired Vince.

"We talked over at Reverchon."

"Huh?"

"He's afraid to go home and is on the run."

"What?"

"He loaded as many of his belongings as he could fit into his Alfa Romeo and is driving to California."

"Has he had any more contact with the Black Widow?"

"No, he's running from her and Veritas. She blackmailed him to supply information on Project Green Field."

"Did Skip confirm that?"

"Yeah, he got in way over his head and couldn't deal his way out. She played on his immaturity and got leverage."

"Well, that certainly explains why he feared getting plugged by Veritas Associates."

"His only move to get out of the hot seat was to resign from National and leave town."

"Anything else I should know about?"

"Skip put his house on the market and left me his key."

Vince paused for a second. "I wouldn't mind doing a walk-through of Skip's bungalow."

"It's getting kind of dark now but you want to go over there tonight?"

"Sure. I can get over there around nine. Does that work?"

"Ok, see you in twenty minutes," I said before hanging up my cell phone and turning onto Mockingbird.

A light mist started to fall as I approached Highland Park. I wondered what would happen to Skip and if he really could extricate himself from this mess.

CHAPTER 33

I turned on my car radio. None of my presets had any music that interested in me so I tuned into the news on NPR. "Earlier this afternoon, Willie Drumingo walked out of San Quentin Prison a free man. He was paroled after spending twenty-five years in prison for killing two young girls in San Diego. His case attracted much attention after he narrowly avoided his date with death in the gas chamber. Since that time, Drumingo's incarceration became a cause célèbre among many influential movers and shakers in the Hollywood community who actively campaigned for his release from prison."

I shook my head and quickly turned off the radio. Had Jim Taggart heard this news? I certainly didn't want to be the one to tell him.

I continued driving. Skip's house was located on the next block so I slowed my car down to turn. As I drove down the street, I noticed a party at one of

Skip's neighbors and all of the parking spots on the street were occupied. The sun had set and Skip's yard and house were completely dark. His driveway was blocked by an illegally parked car so I drove around the next corner and parked. Soon Vince arrived and pulled up directly behind me. We walked to Skip's house and noticed a "For Sale by Flaw Realty" sign planted in the front yard. I fumbled with the key in the darkness as I tried to unlock the front door. Finally, I got the key in the lock and opened the door. I turned on the one very dim light that Skip had left in the living room. Vince turned away from the front door and started checking out some boxes in the living room while I walked back into the kitchen. In a few minutes, I heard the front door slowly open as it squeaked on its old hinges.

"Hello, Skip...we have some unfinished business."

I discretely peered into the living room and saw the Black Widow take two steps forward. I ducked down in order to not to reveal my presence in the kitchen. Now, only her fantastic-looking sinewy legs were visible to me. Vince was partially hidden behind a couple of boxes. Then he stood up and turned to face the Black Widow. They were ten feet apart.

"You're not Skip," the Black Widow said with a disarming smile.

Vince carefully studied her. "But I know you're the Black Widow."

"What? What are you talking about?" she said with a startled look on her face.

"I'm Vince Truex with the Dallas Police and we know all about you. We're going to go downtown and talk about a few things—like the beatings you gave Skip Wise and the blackmail threats."

The Black Widow momentarily looked surprised. Then she grinned, took a couple of steps closer to Vince and said, "I don't think so."

"That's close enough," said Vince as pulled out his Glock 22 pistol and pointed it at the Black Widow.

"You're not going to shoot me." She turned sideways but still looked directly at Vince. Then she slowly turned away and leaned back putting her weight on the back side.

Vince aimed and pulled the trigger. **_Boom_**. The bullet passed two inches away from the Black Widow's face. Her mouth dropped and eyes widened. "Why would you shoot at a lady?" she uttered.

The intense smell of gun powder filled the room. I glanced around the corner but did not reveal my position.

"You're no lady. You're the Black Widow. If you don't get on the ground in three seconds I'm going to blow one of your great-looking wheels into pieces."

"This is police brutality," said the Black Widow as she lowered herself to one knee.

"I think we are going to want to investigate the beatings you gave Skip."

"That's nonsense. Skip and I are just friends who like rough sex."

"Yeah, sure."

The Black Widow looked around as she went to the floor to be handcuffed. "Besides, it looks like he has moved out and might not be around to press charges."

"We'll sort it out downtown and find out more about you."

I remained in the background as Vince led her out the door towards his police car. At least Skip had probably seen the last of the Black Widow. Of course, Veritas Associates was another story.

I stood in Skip's kitchen and shook my head as many thoughts raced through my head. What kind of mess did Skip drop in my lap? I would have to update Bill and Dan about his monkey business. Project Green Field could be dead. Bill and Dan were excitable and not likely to take the news well—I could only hope that they wouldn't shoot the messenger. My career at National Airlines could be over.

I walked into the living room and paused to glance at the bullet hole in the wall before I turned out the dim light and walked out the door. After the police investigated the shooting, the Flaw Realty Company would have to get someone over to the house to tape and bed and paint the unsightly hole in the wall before the real estate agents did their weekly caravan to view all of the new properties on the market in Highland Park.

CHAPTER 34

I was in the shower by five in the morning. Somebody needed to explain Skip's sordid story to CEO William "Bill" Wolf and President Daniel "Dan" McAfferty. Both of them had very busy schedules and executive assistants that closely guarded their calendars. Nobody could sneak into their offices for a private conversation. My best chance would be to get in early and call them directly. Because of my early departure, State Highway 183 was wide open and I made great time. I called Dan within seconds of arriving in my office. The call rang twice and then I heard his deep voice. "McAfferty."

"Dan, this is Lonny Jones. There are some new developments around Project Green Field that I need to discuss with you and Bill as soon as possible."

"Bill and I are on a conference call with Wall Street in an hour. It's going to have to wait. We have our Project Green Field status meeting this afternoon—tell us then."

"Well, some of the information is of a personal nature."

"Don't worry. Just the senior guys will be there. See you this afternoon."

Then I heard a click and the call was over.

I attended a few budget meetings in the morning and just occupied a seat in the room. My mind drifted elsewhere to the looming discussion about Skip and Project Greenfield with the senior officers of National Airlines. A couple of hours passed and I scribbled a few notes as I ate a greasy hamburger and fries for lunch at my desk. I shut my eyes for a moment to gather myself. The status meeting would begin in ten minutes. I started walking towards the elevator bank for the short ride up to the seventh floor that housed the executive offices and conference rooms. This would be my first update meeting on Project Green Field without Skip. The elevator door opened on the seventh floor and I quickly exited and headed to the executive suite in the north wing. I walked past Dan's executive assistant's desk and glanced over. Uncharacteristically, I was met with a cold stare— maybe she found out I tried to do an end-around earlier? My eyes looked straight forward as I approached the conference room. The door was shut but I could hear yelling behind it. I could make out Bill's distinctive voice, "That's unacceptable. That's totally unacceptable."

That was followed by a couple minutes of silence. Then the double doors flew open and Bill Wolf strode quickly to his office followed by Dan McAfferty who glanced over at me as he walked past. "Get ready, we'll get started in five minutes."

The senior officers were all on their cell phones checking their messages and didn't look up as I sat down directly to the left of Dan's usual seat. Then I connected my laptop to the projector and readied myself. Soon Dan and Bill walked in and sat down. Both men lit a cigarette and the meeting began. Dan looked over at me and said in a very deep voice, "Jones, what is your news about Project Green Field? Where the hell is Skip?"

"I have some bad news."

Bill looked over and flashed his white teeth. "What bad news?"

"Yesterday, Skip asked me to meet him. He was out of sorts and looked terrible."

"Well?" replied Bill Wolf.

"He told me he was resigning and asked that I deliver this to you," I said as I handed Skip's envelope to Dan.

A silence filled the room as Dan quickly read the letter and then handed it to his right over to Bill. All eyes were on me as Dan turned and stared. "Why did he quit?"

"He said he had been compromised. He was blackmailed to provide information about Project Green Field. He thought resigning was his only way out."

"That son of a bitch," screamed Bill.

"Bill, you're absolutely right," echoed Dan as he shook his head.

Bill's eyes narrowed and his white teeth glistened as he looked around the room. "I thought he might be a weak link."

"Why didn't Skip just come to us when this problem came up?" asked Dan as he shrugged his shoulders.

I was not sure if this was the time for me to jump into the conversation but I went ahead. "He was scared to death about Veritas. He thought they were going to kill him."

Bill had a dumbfounded look on his face and briefly paused. "What are you talking about?"

"Do you remember when the two men were caught inside my house and they beat up my dad?"

"Yeah, that was a couple of months ago."

"Skip was convinced that Veritas had figured out that there was a mole. He thought he would be uncovered. He knew they were going to kill him."

Bill and Don exchanged glances and shook their heads. There was dead silence in the room. The other senior executives cowered and looked down. Then Bill looked directly at me. "So you and Skip thought we had hired Veritas Associates to plug the leak?"

"Well, there was rumor that they were on the property last year," I responded.

Dan puffed up his cheeks. "We didn't hire Veritas to find the leak. In fact, we never have hired them. We interviewed them last year but based on advice from our General Counsel Ms. Horvath we didn't move forward. Right?" as he pointed at Renee Horvath at the far end of the table.

She quickly nodded affirmatively and answered, "That's right."

All of the senior officers around the table looked puzzled and said nothing. Bill looked around the room and laughed. "They're loose cannons. We would have hired Veritas if we wanted to overthrow a government."

The room exploded in laughter.

"Or if we wanted to invade a country," added

Dan.

More ruckus laughter followed.

Soon the grin left Bill's face and the laughter quickly died out. "Seriously, we did have concerns about leaks on Project Green Field so I asked Dan to build a negotiating channel to his counterpart at Global and talk directly with him. We kept the Green Field effort going only to confuse those bastards at Northern and let the mole pass erroneous information to them."

Dan grinned and laughed. "We heard about the Veritas rumor last year. But we didn't want to change the perception that a hammer could come down at any time. That keeps people in line."

The seated senior executives exchanged glances and politely laughed as the meaning of Dan's statement began to sink in.

The meeting ended in five minutes and I headed down to my office. Since the burglars had nothing to do with Greenfield or Skip then why were they at my house? Then the obvious answer popped into my head—my good friend Jack Heygood.

CHAPTER 35

Maggie planned to move back to the house today and live with Joe and me. I looked forward to something good happening after all of the recent drama around Skip and the Black Widow. Our initial time back together had gone well so far and I hoped Maggie would want to reconcile. But, surprisingly, I had not heard from her in over a week and wondered if she changed her mind. I needed some exercise and decided to do a workout over at the YMCA. Maybe that would help clear my head, too.

I quickly changed into shorts and pulled a hoodie over my tee shirt. My old, refurbished Schwinn bike stood in the corner the garage covered by an old bed sheet. The tire air pressure gauge displayed sixty pounds so I was good to go and coasted down the driveway. Then I started to pedal over to the YMCA. The temperature was eighty-two degrees. I decided to enjoy the beautiful weather and headed east on the bike lanes that lined Northaven

Road. Ten minutes later I was in front of the YMCA and walked over to the bike rack located near the main entrance. I carried the same chain to lock my bike for the last thirty years. After I secured my bike, I glanced to my left to see a new Fuji racing bike—the sort of high-performance machine that costs more than three grand. Surprisingly, it stood unlocked in the bike rack. I shook my head as I walked into the exercise room.

The weights were to the right and in the back while treadmills and cycling machines lined the left side. The assisted pull-up machine sat directly in front of me. I did four sets, with increasingly more resistance, of pull-ups with palms facing away followed by palms facing each other. The bench press would be next and was always a favorite. Recently, I had to back-off on the weight because of pain in the elbows so I focused on increased repetitions with less weight instead. Several personal trainers worked the room. Many of my friends recommended I get their input but I never did and continued to follow the same workout I used to train for high school football many years ago. A couple of friends stopped by to talk and, as always, the conversation turned to college football. I did a few more exercises and wrapped things up.

On my way out to the bike rack I gave Joe a call at the house. "I just finished pumping iron. Has Maggie called?"

"Nope, nobody has called."

"I'm going to take a ride and should be home in an hour. Let me know if she calls."

"Wasn't she supposed to move back in today?" inquired Joe.

"Yeah, that's the plan. Thanks. I'll see you

later."

I continued east on Northaven and after a few minutes crossed Inwood Road. Soon, the bridge over the Dallas North Tollway stood in front of me. I stopped and looked down at the snarled traffic below. Maintenance work was being done on the right shoulder of the north-bound lane so the traffic merged left. I continued east for another mile and then did a U-turn in the parking lot of the Church of the Flying Saucer. It was time to go home.

After over thirty minutes of strenuous pedaling into a stiff breeze from the west, I finally reached my block and headed north. I passed Maggie's former house and then looked up to see several vehicles parked in my driveway. Shortly, I pulled into the driveway and saw Maggie standing in the back of a rental truck. She looked over at me. "Well, it's about time you got home. I was beginning to think that Joe and I would have to unload it by ourselves."

I walked up the ramp into the back of the rental truck and grabbed a box. "I'm sorry, I wasn't sure you were going to make it."

Maggie smiled. "Well, the truck rental place was busy and I am a little late."

I put the box down and stood directly in front of Maggie. "It's great to see you and know you will be living with us."

"Thank you for inviting me back. I'm here to stay."

I put my arms around her and held her close. Just then I could hear someone walk up the ramp. Joe looked tired. He grabbed another box and started to walk down the ramp but stopped and turned. "Hey, I could use a little help. If you guys could break it up for a few minutes, we could finish and I can get out of here."

Maggie smiled at me. "Let's do it."

CHAPTER 36

One week after the Major League Baseball draft the team assembled to play the first game of the year in a tournament in Addison, a suburb north of Dallas. This would be the beginning of our march to the National Championship Tournament in Phoenix. Last season the Generals had advanced to the championship game but lost to the East Cobb Pelicans in a close game. Coaches Ronnie Espinosa and Stan White had laid the groundwork for a successful season by adding key personnel to the roster to shore up our weaknesses. However, several Generals had been selected in the MLB draft and could sign at any time. Josh Baker, an outstanding two-sport athlete out of Lubbock, Texas was the biggest question mark as he had been selected in the first round of the draft and would command over a million-dollar signing bonus. The Generals' only hope was that he elect to pursue a college football career at California Southern University and not sign a professional baseball contract. Last summer he had stayed at the house with Joe and me but we had not seen or heard from him in weeks.

The temperature was blistering hot for early June in Dallas and forecasted to be over one hundred degrees. Fortunately, this stadium provided covered seating for the fans. Joe and I arrived early and no fans were seated. I glanced around the park. A red brick, three-story, luxury apartment complex provided a backdrop behind both left and right fields. Interestingly, we played our opener in this very stadium last year. Looking around at the surroundings brought back lots of memories. That game was very exciting but overshadowed by the off-the-field events involving Jack Heygood in the parking lot. At the time, Jack was on the run and came out to discreetly watch his son Mark play the game from down the right field line near the wall. However, he had been followed by a couple of thugs who wanted him to return money to some investors who has been swindled in the Tropical Investments Ponzi scheme planned and executed by Jack and the other senior executives. The thugs were in the process of beating up Jack in the middle of the parking lot before I came out of the stands with a baseball bat and intervened. In the ensuing melee, Jack broke free and ran away leaving me alone with the thugs. But for the grace of God and a passing security guard, I could have been killed. Jack later apologized to me several times for the incident and I thought he genuinely felt bad about leaving me in that predicament. Fortunately, it was a new year and all of that negativity was behind us.

I meandered down to the parking lot to get a cool soda out of my ice chest. On the way down the ramp to the street level I glanced over to my left to see Coach Ronnie Espinosa engaged in a passionate embrace with a woman in the shadows of the stadium. Ronnie's tawdry affair with a player's mother last year was the talk of the summer. I did a double take and sure enough the woman with Ronnie was Brock Dillard's mother. There was a rumor going around the team that the Dillards had gone to family counselling at the end of last season but based on the display of passion I just witnessed, it probably had not been successful.

By the time I arrived at the parking lot, several more parents had arrived and were standing together in a group, shaded from the sun, on the east side of the stadium. Murray Sr. and Sofia McClure were the first to greet me. He was a jovial guy with mostly gray hair and a medium build. Sofia had a devilish smile and liked to put her hands on me when Murray was not around but I was never sure of her intentions. She stood 5'8" with shoulder-length brown hair and blue eyes. I quickly shook hands with Murray. He slapped me on the back and said, "Congratulations. Great to hear that you and Maggie are engaged."

Sofia winked at me and laughed. "Somehow I never saw this coming. You and Maggie seem to have lots of ups and downs. I bet there're plenty of unhappy women after you got off the market."

Like many times in the past, I didn't know how to respond to Sofia. Murray looked at me and shook his head. I sighed and said, "Things just worked out for Maggie and me."

I continued on to the Mustang *Bullitt* and the ice chest in the back seat. Just then Brock Dillard's mother walked past me and opened the door to her car. The she glanced over at me. "Well Lonny, good to see you. Are you ready for another season?"

"Yes, but I'm looking forward to Joe moving on to college baseball and the next stage of his career."

"I agree, this youth select baseball scene is a beatdown for parents. Where is Joe going to play next year?"

"He has an offer from Our Savior's; and the Texas University coaches called and said they might have room for him depending on which of their recruits sign pro contracts."

"Ronnie said today that TU always loads up with recruits that are high draft choices and many of them never make it to campus."

I grinned. "Yeah, that's what I'm hoping for."

She looked at me for a few moments as if she wanted to say something but nothing came out of her mouth. Then she briefly closed her eyes. "Ah, by the way, I moved in with Ronnie last month. It's for the best. Brock is staying with his father until he goes to college in the fall."

None of this information surprised me but I didn't expect to hear it from her in a parking lot at a baseball game. I exhaled and tried to gather myself. I smiled and said, "Best of luck to you and your family."

What else could I say? I quickly clutched a can of soda and headed back to the assembled group of parents. I glanced around. Oh no, I just spotted Chester Frizzell. Friz had an intimidating presence as he stood over 6'3" and had a barrel chest. The guy was an insufferable carpet salesman that always bragged about his son Mike's baseball exploits and potential. Mike was a guest player on last year's Atlanta trip and Friz was tossed out of the game

Mike pitched at Georgia Tech for arguing balls and strikes from the bleachers. That tirade gave everyone associated with the Generals a bad name at that tournament. I tried to duck behind a couple of other dads but, unfortunately, he saw me and started walking over. I was trapped. There was no escape. Then I heard the customary, "Jones, how are you buddy?"

"Friz, how's carpets?" I responded.

Sofia McClure stood a few feet away and laughed. Friz shook his head and briefly looked at Sofia before turning towards me.

"Sorry you guys got beat by East Cobb in the final last summer. If Mike had been there it would have been a different outcome."

Trying to change the subject away from the brutal conclusion to last year's season, I said, "Congrats to you and Mike on the scholarship from Oklahoma Tech."

"Well thanks. I appreciate that. But I don't think Mike will ever set foot on campus."

"Huh?"

"The MLB scouts are always watching Mike pitch. He will be in rookie camp by the end of the summer."

"But he wasn't drafted."

"I fully expect an MLB team to offer him a free agent contract this summer. Mike's *The Prodigy...*"

This was vintage Friz and getting increasingly harder to stomach.

I raised my hands. "I hope it works out for Mike."

Then I heard a car honk a couple of times before it pulled up in a close parking spot. In a couple of minutes, Jack Heygood emerged holding a large, red

Solo cup. A statuesque blond wearing sunglasses was on his arm. He walked into the middle of the group and shouted, "Good to see everyone! I'm glad to be back."

Then he proceeded to shake everyone's hand and slap people on the back. It was like watching a political candidate work a crowd. Most people were startled to see Jack, especially after the reports of his demise last year, but he held court and quickly won them over.

Murray McClure walked up to Jack. "So, tell me about your business."

Jack held up his hands for emphasis and his large, red Solo cup passed within a few feet of my nose. Based on the smell, the limes floating on top, and the size of the cup, Jack held a triple gin and tonic. He surveyed his audience and addressed the assembled parents. "I've turned my life around. All I want to be is baseball dad and watch Mark play ball."

Then Jack nodded his head several times and continued. "I stood up an international agricultural company in ninety days after securing venture capital funding. Investors are begging to participate—they're going to have to stand in line."

Jack inhaled deeply. Before he could continue, a dad inquired, "What did you think about the article on your company in the business section of Sunday's paper?"

Jack's face lit up. "I loved the half-page, color picture of me with the boxes of avocados in the background."

Everyone laughed except Chester Frizzell. I wondered if he thought that Jack got too much attention and adulation from the parents. Friz raised his hand and then sarcastically said, "Are we going to have to worry about people shooting at you from slow-moving Chevys this season?"

Jack seemed to outwardly appreciate the humor and laughed. Then he turned and looked at Chester Frizzell. "You know Friz, if your mouth keeps moving I am going to buy the carpet company and fire your ass."

Everyone laughed. Then I caught Jack and Friz quickly exchange a couple of glances—for an instant there were no smiles. Maybe Jack's statement was less of a joke and more of a not so thinly-veiled threat that Friz now clearly understood. His face became expressionless. Jack's Solo cup was empty and he excused himself to go to his car and reload.

Game time was ten minutes away so the parents started moving towards the stands. Then I heard the rumble of a muscle car. I turned to see Josh Baker's red Corvette headed directly towards Jack, now holding a refreshed drink, and me. Josh jumped out and immediately walked over to us followed by his girlfriend. "Mr. Jones, great to see you."

"Josh, congratulations on being drafted in the first round of the MLB draft."

"Thanks, it was an honor."

"Have you signed?"

"No, not yet. They offered one million dollars."

"Ahh…"

Josh's eyes glistened. "I want one million after taxes."

"Do you think you'll get it?"

Josh paused of a second. "Oh yeah, you remember Nick Del Monico?"

I chuckled. "How could I forget him?"

Nick was the sketchy attorney from Lubbock

who officed across the street from the jail and negotiated the red Corvette for Josh from a college in Oklahoma last summer.

Josh continued. "Nick expects to have a deal done by the end of the month."

"Just curious, is your dad involved in the negotiations?"

Josh laughed. "No, Butch will be in the county jail for another sixty days. I will be playing in the minor leagues before he gets out."

We could hear the public address system inside the stadium as the teams were introduced.

"The game is about to start. Are you going to play?"

"No, I don't want to risk getting injured. I'm just here to see my home boys."

Jack had remained silent throughout the conversation but carefully studied Josh. His eyes were getting red and his speech slurred as he extended his hand. "Son, I have heard a lot about you. I like your style."

"Thank you, sir. I enjoyed rooming with Mark over at the Jones' house last summer. You are a legend!"

Jack enjoyed the compliment and a wide grin appeared on his face. Then we turned and headed into the stadium to watch the Dallas Generals' opening game.

CHAPTER 37

The game moved quickly and the Generals were up by ten runs in the bottom of the last inning. I watched the game from behind home plate and the parents and fans of our opponent were seated directly in front and to the right of me. Jack wandered over and sat down. "The Generals are really kicking butt today. I love it. Pick up the song books—this game is over!"

Jack's comments embarrassed me. He took a drink from his red Solo cup and looked over at me. "Winning is everything," said Jack. Then he noticed the disdainful looks from some of the people around him. Jack shrugged his shoulders and shouted, "If you don't believe it you're a loser."

Fortunately, the Generals' season opener was soon in the books and the fans quickly departed the stadium. In ten minutes, Joe and I headed to the Mustang *Bullitt* in the parking lot after the brief post-game meeting. I carried Joe's baseball bag as he sipped a large, energy drink. "Well, what do you think about this year's team?"

Joe momentarily stopped drinking. "We're going to miss Josh Baker. He was the difference maker last season. But we did pick up some new talent and Mike Frizzell had very good command of his pitches today."

"I wonder if everyone will stay focused since college is around the corner."

"Yeah, last year was about impressing the college scouts to get a good scholarship offer. The scouts were at all of our games so you never could let down and take a game off."

Just then Joe's cell phone rang and we stopped walking as he took the call. "Yes, sir. That sounds great...I'm glad that some scholarship money became available...Austin is a great place...Thanks again."

Joe turned and gave me a high-five. "I'm going to play baseball at Texas University."

I was elated. TU was always my favorite college option for Joe. Everything was finally working out. We arrived at the car and I popped the trunk to stow Joe's baseball bag. Then I heard a familiar booming voice. "How 'bout them Our Savior's Comets?"

OSU recruiting coordinator Buddy Johnson stood ten feet in front of us. In a second, we were face-to-face. His prodigious body provided shade from the blazing Texas sun. He reached out and his massive paw engulfed my hand. Buddy turned towards Joe and looked him in the eyes. "The staff is looking forward to your joining the team next season. We think you can contribute right away. There are several scenarios that could thrust you into the starting lineup—either on the mound or in the outfield."

Buddy turned to me. "Of course, Mr. Jones, you are welcome to come to campus at any time. The fall intrasquad World Series is just around the corner in October. We cook burgers after the games and the coaches get to know the players' families."

How should I respond? I glanced at Joe. This was his deal and a time for Daddy to keep his mouth shut. Joe looked at Buddy and paused for a moment. Then Buddy interjected, "I haven't received your signed scholarship paperwork. Is there a problem?"

Joe took a deep breath and began to speak. "Well, there's no problem. TU just offered me a twenty-five percent ride and I accepted."

Buddy looked shocked. His face scrunched up and he briefly looked around. "Have you actually signed the TU scholarship letter?"

Joe shook his head. "They just called with the offer."

A slight smile came to Buddy's face. "Good, let's talk."

"Ok."

Just then Jack Heygood sauntered up carrying his over-flowing red cup and appeared to be feeling no pain. He stood to the immediate left of Buddy and listened intently while stirring the refreshed drink with his right index finger. His face was red from the bright sun and the numerous gin and tonics consumed. Buddy gave him several quizzical glances and then continued his sales pitch. "We teach Christian values at OSU. You will leave a better baseball player and person. Joe, is that important to you?"

Jack raised his eyebrows and started to chuckle as he listened to Buddy. Joe responded, "Yes—"

Buddy took a deep breath and continued before Joe could say more, "Good, that's what I thought."

Then Buddy's eyes shifted over to me. "Mr. Jones, you know what goes on down in Austin. Do really want Joe to be exposed to that kind of environment?"

Before I could respond, Jack laughed and said, "I spent the best five years of my life at TU. It was a helluva ride!"

Buddy gave Jack a scornful look and said, "Just who are you?"

Jack grinned and deadpanned, "I'm *The Jack Heygood*. Some of my investors call me *The Prince of Guacamole*. Who might you be?"

Seeming to enjoy his humor, Jack burst out laughing. Both Joe and I chuckled. Buddy puffed up his cheeks and seemed to be at a loss for words. The he grimaced and said, "Call me if you change your mind."

Then Buddy turned, huffing and puffing, and walked away. Jack, Joe and I were left standing by the *Bullitt* alone in the middle of the empty parking lot. Jack took a drink from his cup as he watched Buddy drive away and turned to me and said, "I hope I didn't say anything wrong."

"No, you were spot on," I replied.

At that moment, I wondered about Mark and his future. I knew this could be a tough conversation with Jack but decided to ask anyway. "What are Mark's plans for next year?"

Jack took a deep breath and another drink from his cup. "I think he's going the academic route but may try to walk on if he has a reasonable shot to make the team."

"Ok."

"He's been admitted to TU's Plan Three Honors Program—the academics will be rigorous. The TU coaches say they'll watch him closely this summer and if they like what they see then they'll offer a preferred walk-on spot. He'll be given a locker like the scholarship players on the first day of classes."

A smile appeared on Joe's face. "Maybe Mark and I can room together down in Austin next year."

CHAPTER 38

The initial one million dollars of seed money provided by respected venture capital firms Blue Ridge Partners and Pine Tree Capital enabled Jack to establish solid footing for the company and demonstrate complex logistics capabilities. So the proof of concept was considered to be a success by all concerned. Now, the investors were clamoring for rapid expansion. The whole venture capital community was now abuzz and other players wanted to become involved. In the initial funding process, Jack's proposal was ridiculed by many because of his checkered past and the complexity of the proposed international operation. The dynamic had changed— Jack could have access to almost unlimited funding provided by a plethora of eager investors. A herd mentality had kicked in and everyone wanted a piece of the action.

Usually the presentations for Series A funding are done privately with prospective investors on a case-by-case basis in each of their offices. However, a bigger and grander stage was deemed necessary by Jack. One of the venture capital firms, Blacklock Partners—that declined to participate in the seed funding—offered the use of an exclusive yacht club in Marina Del Ray. This time when Jack asked me to come with him to California for an investor meeting I didn't ask why but rather why not. Jack spent the last few weeks building and practicing his sales pitch in Jerry's office at the warehouse where he could stand and project his slide deck to Jerry and Johnny Kwon. Now it was time to travel and do the deal.

The National Airlines flight from Dallas to Los Angeles landed twenty minutes late due to the strong head winds from the west. Since Jack and I were sitting in first class there were no worries or complaints as the extra air time enabled us to get another round of drinks before we landed. Unlike our earlier trip, when we drove a car from the cheapest discount rental company, a shiny, black Suburban waited to drive us to our hotel.

The drive north on Highway 1 to the upscale hotel on West Washington Blvd took only ten minutes. A clerk at the front desk greeted us with a smile. Jack pulled out his identification from his wallet and placed it in front of her. "Mr. Heygood, nice to see you. How many are in your party?"

Jack glanced over at me and replied, "Just Mr. Jones and myself."

"Blacklock Partners wanted to be sure you were taken care of on your trip. We have a suite available on the top floor with two bed rooms. How does that sound?"

Jack nodded. "Yes, that works."

We walked over to the elevator bank and Jack pushed the button for the twelfth floor. There were only eight suites on the floor. Our spacious room located in the southwest corner afforded a view of Venice Beach to the west and Marina Del Rey to the south. The fog had started to roll in so our view soon became limited.

Fifteen minutes later the room phone rang and Jack answered. "This is a pleasant surprise...We would be interested...We'll see you downstairs in an hour."

"Who was that?" I said as I turned away from the TV towards Jack.

"Laura Newell."

"Wasn't she the partner at Blacklock that tried to torch you at Demo Day?"

"Yes, but now she is anxious to talk," said Jack as he put his feet on the coffee table.

"Didn't you tell me that the two of you had a brief affair over a long weekend in Las Vegas?"

Jack nodded. "It didn't end well since she was blamed for recommending that Blacklock Partners take an equity stake in Tropical Investments just before the crash."

"Her professional career probably took a hit over that?"

Jack raised his eyebrows. "Yeah, so did her personal life."

His response got my attention. "What do you mean?"

"She was engaged to be married a couple of weeks later but her fiancé didn't completely trust her and had her tailed by a private detective. He took some real high-quality, color pictures from the air vent. So that kind of put the kibosh on her nuptials."

I shook my head in disbelief. "Sometimes events like that end really bad."

"Yeah, he had no sense of humor and got real hot. All she was trying to do was sow some wild oats before she settled down. Needless to say, I looked over my shoulder for several months after that episode."

This upcoming dinner meeting with Laura Newell felt like a disaster waiting to happen. How was I going to get out of this? I looked over at Jack. "I'll tell you what. Why don't you meet Laura by yourself? I can just eat in the coffee shop downstairs."

"No, I don't want you to have to eat alone. Besides, your presence will help keep me out of trouble," responded Jack with a sly smile.

We went downstairs and waited in front of the main entrance for a few minutes. Soon we heard a honk and a green Land Rover rolled up. Jack sat down next to Laura in the front seat while I settled in the back directly behind him. Laura looked over at both of us. "There's a great sea food restaurant near the Venice Fishing Pier. How does that sound?"

"Let's do it," responded Jack.

We continued west on Washington Blvd and the beach and pier were directly in front of us. After parking, we walked a couple of blocks to the restaurant. The area seemed to be a mecca for old weather-beaten hippies wearing tie-dyed shirts. There were shirtless young people on skate boards with multiple rings in their bodies. So this was the California that I had always heard about.

The inside of the posh restaurant had a completely different feel. A very large man greeted us at the door and directed us on into the dining area. I was sure one of his major responsibilities was keeping the riff-raff outside. The maître d' smiled and walked towards us. "Would you prefer an ocean view?"

"Yes, that would be fine," answered Laura.

Jack sat down next to Laura while I sat across the table. The sun began to set and you could barely see the fisherman at the end of the pier. A bottle of wine arrived and our waitress poured us each a glass. Laura raised her glass to toast Jack. "To the continued success of Jack's company."

Jack winked at her. "Thank you, Laura. We feel there is a tremendous upside."

"Blacklock regrets not being involved in the initial round of funding," said Laura with a sad look on her face.

I closely watched the interplay between Jack and Laura. There definitely was some not-so-subtle chemistry between them.

Jack winked at Laura. "I'm sure there will be a role for Blacklock in the future."

I looked down at the table and saw that her fingers were gently caressing Jack's hand. Soon their hands disappeared below the table. They reminded me of a couple of teenagers at the ninth-grade dance. Jack and Laura ordered the shrimp while I went all in and had the lobster. The lobster was delicious and I didn't have room for desert.

Laura looked over at me. "Well, it's getting late. Maybe I should be getting you guys back to the hotel."

"Yes, it's been a long day," I said.

We paid the bill and walked down the street to Laura's Land Rover. As we headed east on

Washington Blvd towards the hotel, Jack leaned over to Laura and said, "You're welcome to come up to the room to talk more about the funding we plan to request."

The natural conclusion of this conversation was obvious. There was never a dull moment with Jack Heygood. Laura pulled into the guest parking garage and we boarded the elevator for the ride up to the twelfth floor. Jack's arm wrapped around her backside. Then Laura laughed. "What's so funny?" asked Jack.

"I haven't gone up to a hotel room with two cute men in a few years," said Laura as she playfully looked over at me.

I laughed to myself and realized that I might have underestimated the scope of her visit. Once we entered the room I turned on the TV hoping that they would soon retreat into the friendly confines of Jack's bedroom. If Maggie caught wind of any of this I would be a dead man walking. Laura made herself at home at the wet bar and poured her and Jack a couple of stiff drinks. As they stood together, I noticed that Laura had inserted her right index finger inside of Jack's belt in the front of his pants and gently tugged at it. In a couple of minutes they disappeared into Jack's bedroom for the rest of the evening.

• • •

My alarm went off at seven o'clock and I quickly rolled out of bed and walked into the living area. Jack was dressed and sat on the couch watching a business report on TV. Copies of his slide deck were scattered on the coffee table in front of him. There was no sign of Laura in the suite.

Jack looked up from his slides. "Let's get some food in a few minutes. We're going to the yacht club at eight-thirty. The presentation begins at nine."

We went down to the coffee shop just off the main lobby and were quickly seated. I couldn't resist asking. "So, how did last night go?"

"I think Laura is now a very satisfied supporter after I presented the hard facts," said Jack with a chuckle.

Soon our waitress came to our table holding a couple of cups and a carafe filled with coffee. She was striking—a great tan, big blonde hair and a cute smile. She leaned over and asked, "Would you gentlemen care for some coffee this morning?"

Jack didn't look up and appeared to be totally focused on the menu. I looked over at him. "The waitress is here. Do you want coffee?"

Jack quickly looked up at the waitress and his jaw dropped. Then he gazed at her from head to toe. You could hear him exhale. Jack nodded affirmatively. "Yes, please. We're in a hurry so we'll order now. I'll have a couple of scrambled eggs and some toast."

Jack's response to the waitress surprised me. Usually, he would try to exploit any attractive opportunity presented, but today he was totally locked-in on his presentation to the venture capital community.

The waitress glanced over at me. I quickly responded, "The same for me. Thanks."

We quickly downed our first cups and I refilled Jack's cup and mine.

I was still a little bit surprised by the format for Jack's Series A funding pitch since it would be made to a large group of investors at one time. I glanced over at Jack. "Aren't presentations for Series A funding usually done privately with prospective investors. Why are you pitching to such a large group?"

Jack looked up and smiled. "The investor community is very excited about this opportunity. Everyone wants a piece of the action. I want them to see and feel their competitors' excitement to drive the best possible deal for us. If it turns out to be a bidding war then so much the better."

I shook my head—that was a Jack Heygood move. He momentarily placed his cup on the table and laughed loudly.

We quickly finished eating and headed back upstairs. Jack did a couple of dry runs of his presentation before we left for the front entrance. The same black Suburban pulled up and we headed south for the short ride to the yacht club located between Basins B and C. Marina Del Rey was quite scenic with the hundreds of moored sailboats. I lowered my window to enjoy the refreshing ocean breeze. The yacht club looked impressive with a circular driveway and lush flower beds in front. A large flag pole that looked like a mast from a ship stood centered in the front lawn. We pulled around in front and were greeted by Vic Moskowicz from Blue Ridge Partners who quickly ushered us into a large conference room with a podium set up in front on an elevated stage. Jack immediately headed for the podium while I found a seat towards the back and on the side of the room next to the window that afforded a view of the boats adjacent to Basin B.

Some familiar faces filed into the conference room. Pete Stubbs and Tim Jett of Pine Tree

Capital, Billy Jack Kimball and Laura Newell from Blacklock Partners, Vic Moskowicz from Blue Ridge Partners had all attended Demo Day months earlier. This opportunity had gotten too big for angel investors and only the large venture capital outfits had the financial muscle to play. In addition to the firms that attended Demo Day, many other venture capital firms were represented and some had an international flavor. However, this time I couldn't refer to a program with the complete list of attendees. At eight fifty-nine the lights dimmed and the overhead projector turned on. The crowd quieted down as Jack readied himself behind the podium. Then the first slide in Jack's presentation projected on the screen.

"I'm happy to announce that our proof of concept is a total success. Let's review the Team's accomplishments over the last four months. First, we raised seed capital to conduct a proof of concept...Second, we were able to stand up an international agriculture supply company."

Jack paused for a moment as if he were trying gauge the venture capitalists' interest and excitement. "We negotiated very favorable purchase agreements with growers in Mexico and obtained access to distribution facilities...We created a shipping capability...and entered into a preliminary agreement to supply the BEB Grocery Chain in Dallas."

Jack advanced the presentation to the next slide. "Thirty tons of avocados from the fields in Mexico were transported to our distribution facility in Michoacán for processing and packaging. We shipped the product by refrigerated truck on to our Dallas facility before delivering to our happy customer in Dallas. Our logistics capabilities were validated."

Jack stopped speaking and looked around the room as he made eye contact with the VCs seated in the front row. Then the next slide appeared on the screen. "So what is our secret sauce? We have an agile and aligned leadership team—from the operations managers to our investors... We have industry-low unit costs...We focus on providing only the highest quality product to our customer."

Jack paused and looked around the conference room. "Are there any questions at this point?"

No hands were raised but a number of investors nodded their heads approvingly. "Let me now provide you some customer feedback directly from BEB senior leadership," said Jack as he read the four bullets on the screen. "We are able to get as much product as we want when we want. Product received was of the highest quality with little quantity lost due to spoilage. Jack Heygood is a very good partner. We hope to expand our relationship in the near future."

Jack paused and slowly nodded his head in agreement. "I reported this information to the investors last month. But now I have an exciting update on our strategic relationship with BEB. We have already scaled up our operation to accommodate an expanded supply agreement with BEB—we now supply all of their stores in North Texas."

A brief smattering of applause followed that Jack seemed to relish for several seconds before he continued. "Let's move on to our roadmap. Based on the favorable feedback received to date from BEB, we plan to grow our operation as follows: first, we will become BEB's supplier in Texas, then the Southwest and finally the nation. Of course, all of this depends on the continued flawless implementation of our growth plan."

Jack took a drink of water from the cup on the podium and gazed at the assembled group of investors. "Let's discuss funding. Seed funding of one million dollars was provided by Blue Ridge Partners and Pine Tree Capital. They have told us that our performance has far exceeded their expectations."

Jack purposely paused and looked to the audience for validation. Vic Moskowicz and Pete Stubbs nodded vigorously.

"Now, both of these investors want to double down and participate in the next round of funding. Additionally, Laura Newell, from Blacklock Partners, recently expressed a very strong interest in working closely with me and participating in the next round of funding."

Jack's reference to his one-night stand with Laura amused me and I glanced over to see a broad smile on her face.

Jack continued, "Our accomplishments—to stand up the company, make a profit and scale up the operation—already reflect the types of capabilities usually developed through Series A rather Seed funding...Ladies and gentlemen, we are ahead of schedule."

Murmurs could be heard throughout the room. Jack flipped to the next slide. "We are here today to talk about Series A funding. However, to date, we have developed a very profitable business model, expanded our market reach and are in the process of scaling fast and wide. This progress is more commensurate with Series B or C funding. As a result, our funding ask is twenty million dollars for a thirty percent stake in the company."

The presentation ended. Vic Moskowicz stood up, walked onto the stage and held up his hand to get the audience's attention. "Jack, thank you very much. Once again, you have demonstrated a Midas touch," said Vic as he turned to the seated audience of venture capitalists. "The ownership group will receive investor proposals for the next two weeks. We will announce the winning proposals soon after that. Thank you. Thank you very much."

Jack gathered his materials and stuffed them into his briefcase. Then Vic and Pete Stubbs ushered us to the circular driveway and the waiting black Suburban. Vic pulled Jack aside and whispered, "We're going to exercise our pro rata rights in the next round of funding so our stake will not be diluted."

Jack nodded. "You've added a lot of value and provided strategic guidance. I'm glad you're maintaining your influential equity stake."

We shook hands and climbed into the Suburban. Jacked breathed hard and closed his eyes for a several seconds. Then he looked over to me just as we pulled onto Washington Blvd for the short ride back to the airport. "Well, how did I do?"

I laughed for a minute. "You were outstanding!"

Then Jack smiled. "Yeah, I agree."

CHAPTER 39

Jack was exhausted after returning from the long trip to Marina Del Rey and went to bed early but tossed and turned. The latest avocado shipment was scheduled to arrive from Mexico around noon today. But twelve hours had passed and the shipment had not arrived and there had been no communication from the driver. Sunny's head was nestled on his chest and his right arm was around her.

"Jack, why can't you go to sleep?" said Sunny as she caressed his chest.

"I've been thinking about something at work. Maybe I've got a problem."

"What can you possibly do about it at this time of night?"

"I think I'm going to go down to Jerry's warehouse and see what's going on. Do you want to come?"

"No thanks. I am so tired after we made love. I'll stay here. Be back soon, ok?"

Jack squeezed Sunny. "Maybe when I get back we can do it again."

Sunny smiled and turned on her side. Then she looked up. "Who's going to be at the warehouse at this hour?"

"Probably two or three workers and Johnny Kwon, the grave shift manager. He'll probably want to go out for a free breakfast," said Jack with a laugh.

Jack quickly threw on some shorts and a Longhorn tee shirt and headed for the door. He walked barefoot and didn't make a sound as he went outside. He heard a sound to the left and saw a shadow of a man in his neighbor's yard that quickly disappeared. His car was parked on the curb in front and he opened the trunk and pulled out a pair of tennis shoes. The ride to the warehouse took only ten minutes since there was no traffic on Loop 12 except for an occasional drunk driver. As he turned into Jerry's parking lot, Jack noticed a car one hundred yards behind him. It stopped and the lights went out. Jack walked up the steps of the loading dock and into the warehouse. Then he heard a voice with a heavy Korean accent, "Okay pal, stop right there."

Johnny Kwon stepped out of the shadows brandishing a .38. "Oh Jack, it's you. This is a high crime area and I didn't expect you."

"Johnny, have you heard anything from the driver who was supposed to be here at noon?"

Johnny stuffed the revolver in the back of his slacks and said, "He blew out a couple of tires south of Austin and had to be towed to a garage. His radio had a problem. That's all fixed now. I expect him to arrive within the hour."

"So everything is ok," remarked Jack.

Johnny nodded once. "Would you like to eat some late dinner or early breakfast?"

"Great idea, let's go. My car is just outside.

As they went out through the loading dock door, a stocky man ran away from Jack's car. Johnny pulled out his .38 and fired a couple of rounds at the fleeing figure. "Those damn punks. The only thing they understand is the business end of a gun. They'll think twice if they have to pull some lead out of their ass."

"There's nothing to steal in my car," said Jack with a laugh.

Johnny opened the passenger-side front door. "You know Jack, you have to lock your car in this part of town."

Then Jack's cell phone started ringing. The call was from Mexico so he decided to answer. "Hello, Jorge. Could you please hold?" Then Jack turned to Johnny. "You go and bring some food back here. I have to take this call."

Jack reached into his pocket and tossed his car keys over to Johnny as he turned to walk back into the warehouse. Johnny walked around the car and got in. He turned the key in the ignition. ***Boom***, ***Boom***. A flash lit up the sky followed by a fireball as Jack's car exploded near the loading dock. The force of the explosion knocked Jack off of his feet and he fell behind a couple of wooden pallets. Jack remained motionless on the ground hidden from the street by the pallets. In thirty seconds, a car with two men inside drove by on the street and slowed down to briefly observe the inferno. The car stopped and a tall, bald man stepped out to survey the situation. In seconds, he jumped back in and the car sped away at a high rate of speed.

Jack still clutched his cell phone in his left hand. He could hear "Hello, amigo. Que pasa?"

"Somebody just blew up my car. They were trying to kill me. I need to get out of here. Adios!" screamed Jack.

Jack went to speed dial and clicked Lonny's number. The phone rang six times and then the call went to voice mail. Jack hung up and dialed Lonny again. This time he picked up on the fourth ring. "Jack, why in God's name are you calling me at one in the morning?"

"I am at Jerry's warehouse. Someone stuck a bomb in my car. Johnny is dead."

"Stay right there. Don't let anyone see you. I'll call Truex and get back to you shortly."

Ten minutes passed and then Jack's cell phone started to ring. He answered in a muffled tone standing in the shadows on the side of the warehouse next to the pile of discarded old furniture and paintings. "Lonny, what should I do?"

"Truex will pick you up in the back of the warehouse in five minutes. Remain out of sight until he gets there. You will know it's him because his lights will be out. Stay low when you sprint to his car."

In a few minutes, the Dallas Fire Department arrived on the scene and extinguished the car fire. Three of the warehouse workers were outside talking to the police that just rolled up. Jack quietly snaked his way through the pile of junk on the side of the warehouse towards the back. Then he positioned himself behind a hedge that faced the street to wait for Truex. Moments later a slow-moving car moved down the street without any lights on. Jack broke from the hedge in full stride as Truex opened the back door on his side of the car. In a few seconds, Jack went airborne and dove into the back seat of the moving, unmarked police car. Truex hit the gas pedal and his car disappeared into the night.

Vince Truex drove several more blocks down the street before he stopped to pull over. Then he looked into the back seat. "Heygood, you're a real pain in the ass."

"Thank you for picking me up. Thank you," said Jack as he gasped for air.

"Did anyone see you after the explosion or know you're alive?"

"No, I was out of sight when a car with two men in it passed by just after the explosion. By the time the workers got outside I was hidden on the side."

"Good. Kwon's body was burned beyond recognition and blown to pieces. It will probably be a few days before the medical examiner figures this out."

"So what does that mean?"

"Whoever planted the bomb probably thinks you're dead. Let's leave it that way. Maybe that will help us to figure it out."

"How do I stay safe and not be seen? US Marshalls were supposed to be guarding me. Where the hell are they?"

Truex looked over at Jack and laughed. "You can be safe and tucked away as a guest of the department."

Jack's jaw dropped. "Are you talking jail?"

"Nothing but the finest for you," said Truex with a laugh.

CHAPTER 40

"Mr. Stephens, call on line one. It's the Dallas FBI."

Al Stephens sat behind his massive desk in a corner office at the Department of Justice and briefly looked out of the window that overlooked Constitution Avenue before he responded. "What do they want? Do you know?" Al barked at his secretary.

"Something about Jack Heygood."

"Ok, put them on," said Al as he picked up his phone.

Al rocked back in his desk chair. "Stephens here."

"There are reports that Jack Heygood was assassinated early this morning. A bomb went off in his car and the body was burned beyond recognition. The medical examiner is trying to make a positive identification but it is going to be difficult."

"Oh no. I had William Clayton by the short hairs. Heygood was going to be my star witness in his retrial. As much as I hate Heygood, I have to admit he was a hell of a witness in the first trial. He had the jurors eating out of the palm of his hand. Now, what the hell am I going to do?"

"I don't know, sir."

"Try to keep a lid on this. I am going to try to do a deal with Clayton's counsel, D. Clarence Shapiro. If anything else comes up let me know right away."

Stephen's secretary peered inside his office. "Mr. Stephens, is there anything you need me to do?"

"Get D. Clarence Shapiro on the line."

Twenty minutes later the secretary opened the door to Stephens' office. "Mr. Stephens, I have D. Clarence Shapiro on the line."

"Patch him in."

Stephens sat down at his desk and picked up the phone. "Hello, Clarence. Long time no talk."

"Al, it's always a pleasure."

"How was your vacation to the Cape? I just love the sea food and the weather."

"Fantastic. I even got to watch a few games in the Cape Cod Summer League that is just starting up."

"Outstanding...Regarding the Clayton case, I've been thinking that Clayton has been through a lot over the last few years. I wonder if the best solution for him and this country would be to avoid a costly retrial. I would be amenable to his pleading guilty on lesser charges for a substantially reduced prison term."

"Al, that's a very generous offer. But why would you want to offer that deal when you have such a compelling witness as Jack Heygood who was a Tropical Investments insider?"

"Heygood is a flake but this is really about

saving the tax payers a lot of money."

"I very much appreciate the offer but I think we will pass and take our chances with Heygood on the stand. But, of course, if you were to offer to reduce Clayton's sentence to time already served then we might be able work something out. That would be fair to my client and allow the government obtain a guilty verdict."

Stephens' face reddened and he shook his head in disgust. "Clarence, I am sorry we weren't able to work something out. See you at trial."

Stephens threw down his phone that bounced off the stand on his desk and looked at his chief of staff. "That arrogant son of bitch Shapiro must know Heygood is dead. Clayton must have put out a contract on him. Now what the hell am I going to do? Without Heygood, we can't obtain a conviction. We are going to look like idiots."

Stephens' chief of staff repositioned himself in his chair. "Well, we could accept Shapiro's proposal. It wouldn't be a big victory for the department but a victory none the less."

Stephen's face turned beet red and he growled, "We don't have enough perfume to make that smell good."

The chief nodded in agreement. "Yeah, that was a bit of a stretch."

Stephens stood up and screamed, "Do something useful and get on the phone to the Dallas Police. Talk to Lt. Vince Truex. He has been around the fringes of the Heygood investigations for several years. Also, call Jim Taggart, Heygood's attorney."

"I'll get on it right away, sir," said the chief of staff as he hustled out of the room to avoid Stephens' wrath.

Stephens turned and yelled, "You better come up with something. This mess could tarnish my legacy!"

• • •

There was a loud knock on Al Stephens' office door.

"Come in."

Al's chief of staff entered. "We have a conference call with Truex and Taggart in five minutes."

"What information do they have?"

"We'll find out in a few minutes."

Shortly, Stephens secretary announced, "Mr. Stephens, I have Mr. Taggart and Mr. Truex on line one."

Stephens took the call with his speaker phone. "Jim and Vince, thank you for calling. Let me cut to the chase. I have heard stories that Jack Heygood's car was blown up last night. Do you know anything about his whereabouts?"

"This is Vince Truex. I picked up Heygood last night after the bombing. He is not hurt but one of his associates is dead. Heygood is currently in protective custody in the Dallas County Jail."

Stephens glanced at his chief of staff. "Great news. This is music to my ears. I'm going to kick D. Clarence Shapiro's ass."

After a brief pause, Truex continued, "Two men were seen at the warehouse after the explosion. We have reason to believe that these are the same two men who broke into Lonny Jones' home, assaulted his father and tried to plant surveillance equipment."

"What does this Lonny Jones have to do with

anything?" inquired Stephens.

"Taggart here. Jones visited Jack at the prison in Huntsville. Jack requested that he contact me to represent him in the negotiation with you. He was with me when I negotiated with you."

Stephens paused for a moment. "Based on my earlier conversation with Shapiro, I have no solid proof but only a hunch that Clayton was somehow involved in the bombing."

"What do you want me to do with your witness?" inquired Truex.

"I want you to deliver him to me in Atlanta. At the right time, I will let Shapiro know that Jack is still alive. I am going to enjoy watching him crawl to me on broken glass."

"Will you provide a plane to transport Jack?" asked Truex.

"No, I want to keep this confidential—just you two and only those others that must know in the Dallas Police. I don't have much confidence in my Dallas office—the US Marshalls were supposed to be guarding Heygood. There could be a leak and then a likely second attempt to kill him."

"So, I guess we drive him," remarked Truex.

"Have him in Atlanta in two days. Thank you, gentlemen—"

"One other thing," interjected Jim. "I visited Heygood this morning. The stress is taking a toll. He shook uncontrollably and said he is afraid of dying. He may not be a credible witness."

Stephens stood up and gritted his teeth. "For God's sake. Do whatever it takes to get him to Atlanta. Have his friend Lonny Jones come too if it will help calm him down."

The call ended and Stephens looked at his chief

of staff. "Once we get a look at Heygood in Atlanta we'll need to make an assessment and decide how we want to proceed with Shapiro. They don't know we are holding a wild card. I want a good deal but I don't want to over-play my hand. I'll call an audible at game time."

"That's a great strategy, sir."

Stephens shook his head. "This is not my first rodeo!"

"Yes, sir. I'll make our travel arrangements."

CHAPTER 41

Jack Heygood curled up on his bed in a solitary confinement cell at the Dallas County Jail. Hearing a sound at his cell door, he jumped up. The guard looked in. "Heygood, you have a visitor."

Heygood looked perplexed. "How could that be? Nobody is supposed to know I'm here."

Jack was handcuffed and then escorted to the visiting area. He looked through the glass window and saw Jorge Tatis, Jr. Jack sat down and they both picked up their phones.

Jack rocked back and forth in his chair. "Jorge, how did you know I was in jail?"

"Ramirez told me. He knows everything."

Jack's eyes danced back and forth rapidly. "What?" said Jack incredulously?

"Señor Jack, you have done a lot. Raised the seed money. Started the business. Proven the logistics capability that Ramirez covets. We had such great hopes."

"What do mean—had such great hopes?"

Jorge played with the end of his mustache. "My friend, you're now a liability."

Jack's jaw dropped. "Huh?"

"You have brought much unwanted publicity to the operation. Your car exploded thirty feet from the warehouse. The warehouse manager was blown into pieces. People are digging into your background. Investor perceptions have changed. Your seed investors are scared and want out. What else are you involved in? You worry Ramirez."

"Wait a minute...I built the business," stammered Jack.

"Ramirez has decided you are going to sell the business to him."

Jack shook his head in disbelief. "What?"

"We've already contacted Blue Ridge Partners and Pine Tree Capital. They're eager to liquidate their positions soon and sell to us for a very modest profit."

"What about me?"

"Ramirez will make you a very fair offer and you will accept."

"What if I don't?" retorted Jack.

"We want you to stay healthy... Avocados aren't the end game now that Ramirez is running the show."

Jack looked over at Jorge and mustered a smile. "You know Jorge, avocados were never the end game."

Jorge nodded knowingly and stood up to leave.

CHAPTER 42

Truex parked his police car in the loading area of the North Tower Detention Facility on West Commerce Street. We planned to pick up Jack at five in the morning under the cover of darkness and start the twelve-hour ride to Atlanta. Earlier, Jim Taggart and I met Lt. Truex at the Dallas Police Station and transferred our belongings to his car. We really didn't know what to expect on the trip except we knew that someone wanted Jack Heygood dead. William Clayton was a man of substantial means and capable of financing a hit. If the assassins who blew up Jack's car knew he was alive then there would likely be a second attempt. We didn't want to take any chances so we were armed to the teeth. Truex loaded two M4 carbines that he had checked out from the police gun vault into the car at the police station and each of us carried a Glock pistol. Jack had been under a lot of stress and we didn't know his state of mind. Taggart and I waited in the car for Truex to emerge from the jail with Jack. Finally, at five fifteen the door opened and Vince and Jack jogged to the car.

Jack sat in the back seat with Taggart while I sat in the front with Vince. An eerie silence filled the car as Vince headed through Dallas towards Interstate 20 for the long drive to Atlanta. Shreveport was one hundred-ninety miles east. We planned to eat breakfast there at eight o'clock. Taggart and Jack dozed off in the back seat. I couldn't sleep knowing that we could be attacked at any time. The two M4s were within reach in the front seat. Just after we crossed the state line into Louisiana, I heard Jack stirring in the back seat. Then he looked over at Vince and said, "Word got out that I was being held in protective custody at the jail. Even my business partners in Mexico know."

Vince shook his head in disgust. "Yeah, if you offer enough money lots of people are willing to sell information."

Jack laughed. "Something else you guys should know, I'm out of business. You might say it was a hostile takeover."

"When you run with the big dogs you can get bitten at any time," offered Jim Taggart with a sly grin on his face.

Shortly, we exited Interstate 20 and pulled into a roadside diner on the outskirts of Shreveport for breakfast. The sign on the highway promised Cajun cuisine and we were not disappointed when we reviewed the breakfast menu. The waitress served us coffee and quickly returned to the table. "Are you gentlemen ready to order?

Jack's spirits seemed to be momentarily buoyed by the offerings. "I'll take the Seafood Gumbo

Omelette with an English muffin."

"Excellent choice," said the waitress as she took notes.

Taggart ordered next. "The Gumbo and Grits sounds good."

Vince Truex studied the menu for a few seconds. "I'll take Cajun Crawfish Eggs with extra Tabasco Sauce."

I had been up for five hours and breakfast had little appeal. "If it's not too early, I'll take the Blackened Catfish Burrito with some extra jalapeños on the side."

"No problem, honey," said the waitress as she winked at me before departing for the kitchen.

● ● ●

Six hours later, still trying to recover from breakfast, we approached Birmingham, Alabama and took the Interstate 459 bypass south through Hoover to avoid the city traffic. Atlanta was one hundred-forty miles away. Truex's phone started to ring just as we got back on Interstate 20 east of Birmingham. "Truex here."

I drove and could only hear Vince's voice in the conversation.

"Ok, I've got it—75 Ted Turner Drive Northwest. We should be there in two hours."

Then Truex hung up and looked at Jack and Taggart in the back seat. "We are going to drop you off with Al Stephens at the US District Court in downtown Atlanta."

Taggart replied, "Al must be working late today."

"It will be after business hours so we might be

able to get Jack inside without being seen," responded Truex.

The traffic moved at a good clip and we were driving over the speed limit. I looked in the rear-view mirror and noticed a silver car with a black hood trailing us by fifty yards. Then the car moved up towards us at a high rate of speed and the red overhead lights came on. It looked like an Alabama State Police car. Then we heard the siren as the car moved up to just off the back bumper. I slowed down to stop the car on the side of the highway. Truex looked over at us. "I'll do the talking here but stay ready in case this is a ruse."

A man wearing a State Trooper uniform approached the car. He was heavyset with a flattop haircut. I rolled down my window on the driver's side of the car. "You boys were going ten miles an hour over the speed limit. I see you're from Texas. What business do you have here in Alabama?"

Before I could say anything, Truex interjected, "I'm Vince Truex with the Dallas Police. We're delivering a witness to the US District Court in Atlanta."

"Which one of you is the witness?" asked the Trooper.

I pointed at Jack in the back seat.

The Trooper lowered his head to look at Jack and saw the M4s on the front seat. His eyes widened and the expression left his face as he took two steps back away from the car. "Whoa, you've got an armory in there. Why do you need that much firepower?" said the Trooper as he lowered his hand onto the handle of the pistol holstered at his side.

Vince leaned towards the window so the officer could clearly hear him. "Here is my police identification. Call it in. There has been one assassination attempt on the witness already and we anticipate another. I don't want to be stopped out here on the side of the road for a long time. Move."

The Trooper grabbed Vince's police identification and started to walk back to his car. Jim Taggart, sitting in the back seat behind Vince, had the best vantage point and continued to intently watch the Trooper as he sat down in the silver car. I looked back at Vince and noticed the intense expression on his face. He kept his eyes on the Trooper for several more seconds and said, "I think he is talking on his cell phone—not the police radio. Something doesn't look right."

"Keep watching," said Vince as he picked up one of the M4s.

I grabbed my Glock that sat next to me on the front console. Taggart's gun was already in his right hand. Jack's heavy breathing was audible as he trembled in the backseat.

"Why is this happening to me?" uttered Jack as his hands started to shake.

"Jim, shoot him if he starts firing from behind the car. I won't have a shot unless he is on the side of the car," said Vince.

The driver's door on the silver car opened. "He's getting out of the car now," exclaimed Taggart.

My adrenaline started to flow and I thought about my first move in a shootout.

The Trooper continued to walk towards the car. "He's got his hand on his gun. He's got his hand on his gun," exclaimed Taggart.

"Heygood, get your head below the window," commanded Vince.

The color left Jack's face as he crouched down. "I

think I'm going to be sick!"

"Shut up, Heygood," responded Vince.

The Trooper passed the back of the car and was now just behind the back door.

Vince whispered to me, "Move your seat all of the way back and I'll try not to shoot you."

Then I heard the click when Vince disengaged the safety on the M4.

"Lonny, watch his hand. If he pulls the pistol out of his holster, yell."

I shook my head since I was going to be the clay pigeon and likely get hit by bullets from both directions. By the time I could raise my gun to the window to shoot the firefight would be over.

The Trooper now stood directly in front of my side window and handed Vince's police identification back to me. He no longer gripped his pistol. Then he leaned towards the window and saw the barrel of the M4 pointed at him. Perspiration immediately started to flow down his face. Then he yelled, "You're good to go—now get the hell out of Alabama."

Not wanting to wait for him to change his mind, I started the car and we quickly merged into the eastbound traffic. Everyone in the car breathed a sigh of relief as the false alarm was over. We were all on edge and wanted this saga to end. Jack Heygood immediately shut his eyes and went to sleep. A smile appeared on Jim Taggart's face. "I think I went on more enjoyable road trips in college."

The two-hour drive to Atlanta was uneventful and we pulled into the US District Court Building receiving area off of Ted Turner Drive. A US Marshall ushered us up to the fourth floor via the freight elevator and we walked down a long hallway to a secured area with a sign that read "US District

Court Personnel Beyond this Point." Al Stephens and the US Attorney in charge of the retrial of William Clayton awaited us in a corner office.

Jack and I sat down on a couch while Truex and Taggart pulled up chairs.

"I never thought I would be so happy to see Heygood," laughed Al Stephens.

The US Attorney studied Jack for several moments and then said, "We need to know where we stand before the arraignment. Jack, I understand it has been difficult for you after the bombing."

Jack's left eye twitched uncontrollably and his hands moved nervously in his lap. "Tell us where you're at," asked the US Attorney.

Jack opened his mouth to speak but breathed heavily and paused for a moment. Then he started to try to talk, "Ahhhhhhhhh." His speech was incomprehensible and Stephens and the US Attorney exchanged nervous glances.

Al Stephens motioned to one of the US Marshalls standing in the back of the room. "Please take Mr. Heygood down the freight elevator to the holding area in the basement where he will be comfortable and secure."

Jack stood up and walked out with two of the Marshalls. The US Attorney turned to Al Stephens when Jack was out of earshot. "I'm not sure he will be a credible witness."

Stephens grimaced. "Yeah, he comes off as one-hundred percent chucklehead. Shapiro will carve him up."

"He's not going to be much use to us now. What do you want to do?"

Al squinted his eyes and said nothing for several seconds. "If Heygood testifies in his current condition then we will not be able to get a conviction. Shapiro is not going to deal if he finds out."

"So we need to make Shapiro believe that Jack is willing and ready to testify," remarked the US Attorney.

"Exactly, isn't Shapiro coming over here for a meeting with you tomorrow?"

"Yes, at ten in the morning."

"Good, let's make it happen."

CHAPTER 43

Two large, black Chevy Suburbans pulled up at the curb in front of the main entrance to the US District Court Building. D. Clarence Shapiro and his entourage of attorneys and support staff exited and headed up the steps. Once inside, Shapiro walked over to the main desk manned by three uniformed security guards. "I have an appointment with the US Attorney regarding the William Clayton matter."

The guard checked the schedule and looked up. "Follow me, Mr. Shapiro."

Shapiro and his entourage squeezed together to fit into one elevator for the ride up to the fourth floor. The US Attorney stood outside of his office in the restricted area to await Shapiro. "Hello, Clarence. Nice to see you this morning."

"Thank you for making the time," said Shapiro as they walked towards the US Attorney's office.

"Could we talk alone for a few minutes? Your staff can make themselves at home in the conference room."

"That's exactly what I had in mind," remarked Shapiro with a grin on his face as they walked inside the office and shut the door.

Shapiro and the US Attorney sat across from each other on opposite sides of the coffee table. There was a knock on the door. Then Al Stephens entered and extended his hand to Shapiro. "Nice to see you Clarence."

Shapiro stood and looked Stephens in the eye. "Great, I always like to negotiate with the top dog."

The three men chuckled for a moment and then the smile left Shapiro's face. "First, I want to thank you for offering the very generous plea deal. However, unless you are willing to offer a sentence of time already served then I want to move forward with the trial. William Clayton favors going forward with the trial anyway to clear his good name."

"Does your client understand the benefit of pleading guilty to lesser charges and receiving a reduced sentence of ten years in prison?" asked Al.

"His legal team is much more formidable now and he trusts our ability to obtain an acquittal on all charges."

"But the government was able to convict him before by offering some very compelling testimony."

Shapiro rocked back in his seat. "That was then and this is now. Are you sure the testimony will be as compelling this time?"

Stephens maintained eye contact with Shapiro. "I have complete faith in Jack Heygood."

"I guess I will have to deal with Mr. Heygood when he appears," said Shapiro with a slight smirk on his face.

The conversation in the US Attorney's office

continued as Shapiro's legal team set up camp in the conference room. The conference room door stood ajar as several team members helped themselves to the free coffee and donuts in the outer office. Two of Shapiro's lawyers hovered over the open box filled with an assortment of colorful iced, glazed and filled donuts. The taller one, holding a full cup of coffee, remarked, "I can't decide between the caramel and the chocolate. Maybe I'll take one of each."

The other lawyer shook his head and grimaced. "Just make up your mind so the rest of us can get one."

A door to an adjacent office opened and a US Marshal looked outside just as the taller lawyer took a big sip of coffee. Then two US Marshalls and Jack Heygood walked through the outer office in front of the entrance to the conference room. The two Shapiro legal team members standing in front of the donut box froze and their eyes widened. The tall lawyer's face turned red, his cheeks puffed up and his eyes moved frantically back and forth for a second before he abruptly leaned over and spit a mouthful of coffee into the pristine box of donuts. All eyes were on Jack. He glanced towards the conference room as he walked by and caught the attention of several others on Shapiro's team. The murmurs from the conference room were audible in the outer office before the door slammed shut.

The private initial discussion between Shapiro and Stephens soon ended and the men stood up. "Let's reconvene with our entire staffs in fifteen minutes," suggested Stephens.

Shapiro nodded. "Okay, I just need five minutes to huddle with my troops."

He walked down the hallway and was met at the

conference room door by the taller lawyer who shook his head from side-to-side and whispered, "We have the worst-case scenario."

Shapiro's face scrunched up as the taller man shut the door behind him.

Sixty minutes later the door to the conference room remained shut.

The US Attorney and Al Stephens waited in the office. Al looked over. "I've got Shapiro by the short hairs if this plays out."

Five minutes later the door to the conference room opened. Shapiro emerged and walked alone back to the US Attorney's office. He briefly knocked on the open door, walked in and sat down to the left of Stephens. "Gentlemen, I discussed the merits of the plea proposal you suggested earlier with my client, Mr. Clayton. After some deliberation, he has authorized me to accept it."

"This is good news for all concerned. I will get some time on the judge's docket to get the plea agreement approved by the court," said the US Attorney.

CHAPTER 44

Al Stephens' press conference was scheduled to begin in ten minutes. We decided to delay our return to Dallas in order to hear Stephens' press conference and allow Jack to get closure on the Tropical Investments chapter of his life. I was thirsty and walked down a darkened, empty hallway towards a drinking fountain. I passed by an office. The door was open and I spotted Al Stephens sitting behind the desk with his back towards me talking on his cell phone. His booming voice was audible in the hallway.

"Yes, sir. This settlement is a total victory for you and the Department of Justice."

A brief pause followed. "Thank you, sir. Yes, I understand. I will keep the mud around Heygood out of your folder."

I got a drink and then headed down the hall towards a large conference room that would host Stephen's press conference. TV cameras lined the back wall. All of the major networks were represented. The standing-room-only crowd awaited Al Stephens. Truex, Taggart, Jack and I stood inconspicuously at the side of the room near the entrance. Jack wore sunglasses to conceal his identity from the throng of assembled reporters. I glanced down at my watch. It was time. Everyone looked towards the entrance as Al Stephens marched in and positioned himself behind a bank of microphones.

Al scanned the crowd with a triumphant grin on his face and then began to speak. "The Department of Justice has reached an agreement with William Clayton's legal team. Mr. Clayton has agreed to plead guilty to ten counts and will serve a ten-year sentence in federal prison. This agreement enables this administration to meet its commitment to the American people—corporate crime will not be tolerated and violators will be prosecuted to the fullest extent of the law. Mr. Clayton's imprisonment will serve as a deterrent to others."

A reporter in the front row raised his hand. "In his first trial, Clayton was convicted on thirty-three counts and sentenced to twenty-five years in prison. The plea bargain included only ten counts and a sentence of ten years. Did Clayton beat the system with this agreement?"

Stephens looked directly at the reporter and scowled. "Mr. Clayton will return to prison. This settlement obviates the need for a costly retrial and saves the tax payers millions of dollars. This is a win-win for this administration and the American people... Next question."

A news correspondent in the back of the room took one step forward and raised her hand. "Now that Jack Heygood will not have to testify, what do you think about his pardon?"

Grimacing, Al Stephens took several deep breaths. "The DOJ has no opinion on Heygood's pardon. That was a Texas matter and a Texas decision. I recommend you direct all questions regarding Heygood's pardon to the Texas Attorney General in Austin."

The reporter smiled but didn't back down. "How do you feel about it personally?"

Stephens paused briefly and adjusted his tie. "Well...personally, I was shocked and dismayed by the decision to grant Heygood a pardon. That's all. Thank you."

Stephens flashed the victory sign as he stopped for pictures and then quickly headed to the elevator being held by his security detail. Jack and I followed Stephens down the hall and stepped in behind him just before the door closed. In a few seconds, Stephens turned to see who was standing behind him and his jaw dropped. Then he turned and faced the back of the elevator. In a loud voice, Jack said, "Why are you not filing murder charges against Clayton?"

Stephens' two burly security guards were soon face-to-face with Jack. Al continued to face the back of the elevator and muttered, "I got what I wanted."

Jack lunged towards Stephens and was quickly in the grip of the guards. He screamed, "What about me? He tried to kill me!"

Then Stephens slowly turned and looked directly at Jack. Their faces were only inches apart. Stephens smiled and Jack's eyes widened. "Mr. Heygood, you must be confusing me with someone who gives a shit."

In a few more seconds, the elevator reached the garage level and the door opened. Stephens walked towards his waiting limousine as his security detail blocked Jack from exiting the elevator.

CHAPTER 45

Housecleaning started a week ago. Any work today would only involve minor clean-up and final preparation. Joe mowed the grass and I cleaned up the patio area earlier. Maggie did some last-minute dusting inside. We had invited sixty friends to a party and fifty-five had accepted. The backyard looked better than ever. Flower pots lined the patio. The batting cage—which had been a fixture for ten years—lay disassembled in the garage. Some fresh sod covered most of the bare spots.

The clock on my phone showed three o'clock. I jumped out of the shower and started to dry myself off. The bathroom door was slightly ajar. Then I heard a knock. Maggie opened the door and stepped in. She was already dressed and looked perfect in a blue dress. "Lonny, what do you think? Is this outfit too casual?"

"No, you look fantastic!"

Maggie smiled, took two steps forward and gave

me a kiss. "Will you be ready soon? The caterer will arrive in fifteen minutes."

"I'll have my clothes on in five minutes unless you have something else in mind."

Maggie laughed. "That's a great idea but I don't think we have enough time."

I quickly dressed and headed to the living room when the doorbell rang. The caterer had arrived exactly on time. I opened the door and the company manager extended his hand. "Mr. Jones, it's a pleasure to cater this event."

"Thanks, you guys have a reputation for being the best."

The manager shook his head in agreement. "I understand the wet bar and margarita machine are to be set up on the patio."

"Yes, that's correct."

The manager turned to his associate to provide instructions. Then several men started to unload equipment from the back of a very large truck. The lime green margarita machine and the wet bar were sizeable.

"Let me show you the kitchen."

He followed me down the hall and in a minute we were standing in the middle of the kitchen. Maggie was already in the kitchen and clearing space so the caterer could setup. She looked over and extended her hand. "I have done a lot of planning with your staff. Let's review the menu."

The catering manager pulled a sheet of paper from his notebook. "Let me see, shrimp cocktail and stuffed jalapeños will be the appetizer. Beef tenderloin will be served with rolls, potato salad and slaw. Chocolate mousse cake will be the desert. In addition to the alcoholic beverages, we will offer lemonade and iced tea to drink."

"Yes, that sounds perfect. We expect fifty-five guests."

"We're good. Let me have my team set up in the kitchen and backyard."

"Great, we expect the guests to start arriving around four."

"No problem, we will be ready."

Everything was going to plan. Maggie's daughters and their families were the first to arrive at three-forty-five. A small army of catering staff had quickly set up fifteen tables on the grass to accommodate the guests. Joe walked outside and surveyed the scene. I turned to him. "Maggie and I are expecting fifty-five people—probably the largest party ever at this house."

Joe smiled wryly. "No way, I had one hundred people here last summer with four kegs of beer when you took that business trip to Florida."

"Oh yeah, I remember. The neighbors called the police. Lieutenant Truex came over and shut it down. That was quite the party."

Joe chuckled. I looked at my watch and it was four so Joe and I moved to the front to meet the guests. Fifteen people from National airlines arrived almost at the same time. A few of them quipped that they were the on-time machine. Twelve co-workers from Maggie's company trickled in. Then Jim Taggart arrived in his Mercedes 450 SL and found one of the few remaining parking spots close to the house. He walked up to me and extended his hand. "Lonny, thank you for inviting me. This is going to be a lot of fun."

"I appreciate you. Thanks for coming. The wet bar is in back with the margarita machine."

Jim waved and headed to the back of the house. Then Vince Truex arrived. He had parked down the street at the end of the block. We shook hands and Vince had a big smile on his face. Before he could say anything, I blurted out, "Are you carrying?"

Both of us broke out laughing. Then he retorted, "I stay ready so I don't have to get ready."

More laughter ensued. I glance to my left and saw a familiar figure walking up the driveway—it was Jack. Vince looked at Jack and then at me. "Heygood is bad news, Look out my friend. I am going to get a drink and shoot up your backyard."

Jack had a mischievous grin on his face as he walked towards me. "I thought better of it and left Sunny at the apartment. Haha."

"Thank you. That would have been a show-stopper. Margaritas await you on the patio."

As Jack started to walk to the back of the house, I wondered what he would do next. I turned towards him and said, "Hey Jack, what's the future?"

Jack flashed a wry smile. "Plastics."

I shook my head and laughed. I had heard that line before but couldn't remember where.

My watch showed four-thirty and just about all of the guests had arrived. One coned-off parking spot immediately in front of the house reserved for the Monsignor at Cardinal Mahony Catholic Church remained. I knew him well. His guidance had sustained me when my ex-wife walked out. I waited in front to escort him in. Five minutes later the Monsignor's Buick came down the street and I walked to the curb to remove the cones that reserved his parking spot. He quickly parked and got out. "Thank you for coming."

"It's my pleasure, glad you asked me. It always

feels better to end Saturday with a wedding rather than a funeral."

We walked around to the backyard and the Monsignor ordered a whiskey neat at the wet bar. Maggie and I mingled with the guests for fifteen minutes and then I took her aside so we could speak in private. "You look beautiful."

Maggie blushed. I continued, "Are you ready?"

"Yes, I am."

We walked hand-in-hand to the middle of the patio. I turned to the Monsignor, we're ready."

The Monsignor raised his hand and the guests became quiet. He looked around at the throng of people before he spoke. "We are here for The Celebration of Matrimony between Lonny and Maggie...Let us pray."

Everyone bowed their head and there was a moment of silence.

The Monsignor stood directly in front of us. "Lonny and Maggie, have you come here to enter into Marriage without coercion, freely and wholeheartedly?"

"I have," I responded.

There was a brief pause and Maggie said, "I have."

The Monsignor paused and looked directly at us before he continued, "Are you prepared, as you follow the path of Marriage, to love and honor each other for as long as you both shall live?"

"I am," we both responded.

"Are you prepared, to accept children lovingly from God and to bring them up according to the law of Christ and his Church?"

I started to breath hard and glanced over at Maggie. "I am."

Maggie smiled at me and then looked forward. "I am."

The Monsignor nodded. "Since it is your intention to enter the covenant of Holy Matrimony, join your right hands and declare your consent before God and his Church."

We, or rather Maggie, decided we needed to write our own vows because of our special relationship. After several weeks of editing drafts, we finally settled on the vows that worked best for us.

I felt light-headed and tried to compose myself. Vince Truex, standing directly to my left, gave me a concerned look. Then I took several deep breaths. "I, Lonny, take you, Maggie, to be my wife, loving what I know of you, and trusting what I do not yet know. I eagerly anticipate the chance to grow together, getting to know the person you will become, and falling in love a little more each day. I promise to honor, love, and cherish you all the days of my life."

Maggie squeezed my hand momentarily and smiled. "I, Maggie, take you Lonny, to be my husband, loving what I know of you, and trusting what I do not yet know. I eagerly anticipate the chance to grow together, getting to know the person you will become, and falling in love a little more each day. I promise to honor, love, and cherish you all the days of my life."

Then the Monsignor confirmed our vows. Following a short blessing, I placed the wedding ring on Maggie's finger. She gazed at her ring momentarily and then placed a ring on my finger. Soon the wedding concluded with the Lord's Prayer and a blessing.

The service had lasted twenty minutes and I felt

relieved and ready to celebrate. I put my right arm around Maggie and pulled her close to me. Our guests started to eat and refreshed themselves at the wet bar on the patio. We walked from table to table around the backyard and thanked everyone for coming.

An hour later, the party started to thin out as our guests began to depart. Surprisingly, Jack Heygood walked out of the backyard without saying goodbye—he was the kind of guy that usually entered and exited parties with great fanfare. Soon, only our closest friends and family remained. Maggie held her grandson and I sat down at a table near the patio with Pete and Joe. Pete smiled. "Son, I'm so happy for you and Maggie. She is the right woman for you."

Joe grinned. "I wasn't sure you could pull it off, but good job, Dad."

I sipped my Coors beer and looked up to see Jack Heygood walking back into the backyard. He carried what appeared to be a large, brown grocery bag. Jack stopped near the gate and motioned me to come over. Pete gave me a concerned look and whispered, "Watch yourself, son. Jack Heygood is nothing but trouble."

I laughed and walked over to Jack standing next to the fence. Jack looked over at me and then slapped me on the back. "It's been a helluva year and I appreciate everything you've done for Mark and me."

I nodded. "Jack, thanks for coming tonight."

"My pleasure," said Jack as he handed the brown grocery bag to me. "This is a present for you and Maggie."

I looked into the bag and studied the contents.

My jaw dropped. It was filled with hundred-dollar bills. "There must be fifty thousand dollars in here. I don't know what to say."

Jack grinned. "Buy something nice for Maggie."

"Thanks, Jack."

Jack waved and started to walk out of the backyard but quickly turned and looked at me. He paused for a moment and winked. "Don't worry, none of the bills are marked."

THE END

ACKNOWLEDGMENTS

A heartfelt thank you to the many people who provided feedback on earlier drafts: Dae Lee, Kevin Beck, Mabel Kung, David Parham, Becky Hopson, Byron Beck, Robert Dees, and three readers who wish to remain anonymous.

Michelle Josette provided an editorial review and copy editing. Her many suggestions significantly improved the novel. Pictures were provided by Brian Dunlap.

PHILIP BECK

ABOUT THE AUTHOR

Phil published his debut novel, *Fastball,* in December 2017. He has held leadership positions in Analytics, Finance, Maintenance and Technology at two major airlines. Previously, he taught and conducted research in academia.

He spent all of his spare time—when not watching baseball—over the last ten months writing *Heygood Gambit,* the second book in the *Fastball Series*.

Author website: https://philipobeckwriter.com

Phil lives in Dallas with his family.

Made in the USA
Columbia, SC
11 December 2018